Going Long

Cari Quinn

ISBN: 978-1-940346-17-5

Editor and Digital formatting: Late Nite Designs
Cover artist: Valerie Tibbs
Print formatting: Kim Brooks

DEDICATION

To my mom, who never stops believing.
To Taryn Elliott, who is my eleventh hour cheerleader and
never lets me panic.
This ride is a million times more fun with you.

PROLOGUE

The road stretched ahead of Wade Bennett, winding up into the mountains of Truxton, Tennessee. Endless miles of land surrounded him, offset by the bucolic farms tucked into the forest. Trees rose up around him like sheltering angels that dripped shade onto the sunbaked earth, offering snatches of respite from the sweltering heat.

He tipped back his coffee mug and took a long sip. June in the south meant sweet tea, and lots of it. It also meant sticking his elbow out the window and soaking up the summer breeze that barely cooled the sweat clinging to his skin.

Behind the wheel of his beat-up old pickup was his favorite place to be. With his dog Melody's head in his lap and the radio blasting country music, he couldn't think of one other spot on God's green earth more perfect or right for him.

Well, just one. But that was more about the people than the place.

He took a curve too fast, spitting up gravel on the shoulder of the road as he passed the Gruber farm. Clothes flapped on the line next to their charmingly rustic barn, a pretty usual sight in this part of the area. Wade had grown up in Quinn, Texas, a small town where football was king and ranching ran herd on many other occupations, so he felt more than comfortable here. It was in the rhinestone glitz and glamour of Nashville that he felt like an outsider in his scuffed cowboy boots, faded jeans and worn-thin T-shirts.

He'd stopped wearing a cowboy hat when his record company had decided to turn him into country radio's version of a Backstreet Boy. Then they'd told him to lose the hat and the twang and the songs that made him who he was in favor of pop shit.

Not that there was anything wrong with pop. It just wasn't him. He might've stashed his black Stetson in his truck—though it was on his head right now—but that didn't mean he'd changed who he was at the root.

Back home, most of his friends hadn't worn cowboy hats. Some had worn boots, some hadn't. Most had helped their families work the land, but some had avoided the backbreaking parts by pitching the old rawhide every Friday night under the hot lights. "Gotta save the arm" had been Wade's older brother Colton's excuse. He'd done his share around the farm and Coach's ranch, but he'd always managed to disappear when it came to mucking out stalls or milking Bessie. No self-respecting golden boy like Colt wanted to get caught with his head between a cow's legs.

His cell beeped in the ashtray and he sighed. Whoever it was, he didn't want to talk. It might be the waitress he'd hooked up with a couple of months ago. Linda was a sweet girl, but he wasn't anyone's bargain right now for love or anything else.

The other possibilities were record company execs or his manager, and neither was appealing. Stanley thought Wade needed to meet some new songwriters and producers to infuse his music with something edgier. More hip. Basically he was spewing Alliance Records' BS version 2.0.

It was better he didn't answer at all.

His phone went off again and he gave up trying to ignore the insistent chime. Looking didn't mean he had to answer.

An unfamiliar number showed up on his Caller ID and he debated just dropping the cell back into the tray. But curiosity had him lifting his phone to his ear. "Yeah?" he said, fully expecting it to be a sneak attack from the record company.

They'd already sprung a visit with some new up-and-coming songwriter on him for the week after next. The dude was in some kind of rock-metal outfit, for fuck's sake. What did he know about writing country songs?

Wade had said yes anyway, because the fact was, his album sales were down. Lonestar Angel had moved half the units of his previous release, and radio wasn't playing him like they once were. Without tour dates to get him back in front of the fans until the fall when his next unnamed single was scheduled to drop, he had no way of reconnecting with his base.

Maybe new music—music *he* hadn't written—was exactly what he needed, but damn if it didn't sting.

The pause on the other end of the phone ended with the clearing of a throat. "Wade, is that you?"

Wade frowned. The voice was vaguely familiar, like a song he hadn't heard in too many years to count. "Yes. Who's this?"

"It's Joel Rodriguez. From—"

"I know where you're from." Quinn. Joel was from Quinn. Fuck. Had thinking about his old hometown been enough to conjure one of his old buddies? "This is a surprise."

"Not a welcome one, it sounds like." Joel laughed. "Am I calling at a bad time?"

"Yes. No. Shit, let me pull over. I'm on the road."

"Oh, are you on the way to a show?"

The excitement in the other man's voice made Wade grin before the disappointment in himself reared up once again. He wasn't on the way anywhere if he didn't figure out how to up his worth to the record company. "Nah, just driving to clear my head. Trying to come up with some new music. You know how it is." The lie came easily, like so many others had recently.

No, I'm not having trouble coming up with new material.

No, I'm not frustrated, pissed off and bored.

No, I haven't turned my back on this life.

7

That was the biggest one of them all, because part of him had. He'd stopped connecting with the fans when his sense of isolation within Nashville had reached critical mass. Instead of his years in the biz making it easier for him to meet new people, he was retreating into himself more and more. The mask he'd once worn to make it seem like he belonged had fallen away, and he couldn't set it back in place no matter how hard he tried.

"Oh sure. I get it. You creative types need your mental space," Joel teased, his familiar voice tossing Wade into the past so swiftly that he wondered when he'd stepped out of his Silverado and into a DeLorean.

The road in front of him melted away, becoming an acre of shimmering green grass. Joel, the center on the team, flashed Wade a grin as he walked up to the football and prepared to kick. It was an often-thankless job on the squad, but a hasty kick could set the wrong tone for an entire game. Tonight, Wade was feeling good. Ready to do some damage. With the roar of the hometown crowd in his ears, he glanced toward the cheerleaders, hoping to catch a glimpse of Charlene in her short black and silver skirt.

And he did. Oh, he did, but she was smiling at Colt. Pound for pound, a star linebacker was almost always worth more attention than the kicker who played his guitar better than he ran the field.

"You know it," Wade said, steering to the side of the road so abruptly that Melody lifted her head and let out a low yelp. "Sorry, baby." He patted her head and turned off the truck. For once, he didn't want to listen to music.

Not even his own.

"So how've you been?" Wade asked into the silence, surprised to realize his palm was clammier than it had been just a moment ago. "It's been a damn long time."

"Too long. We haven't talked in what, two years? Three?"

"Something like that. Damn shame how time gets away from us."

"It is." Joel sighed. "Look, Wade, this isn't just a social call. I have some difficult news."

Images flashed in Wade's mind. His little sister, Hollie, nestled away in the library, surrounded by books older than she was. Colt, running with those stupid earbuds in his ears, music set on scream. His mama, rocking on her porch swing. His pop, working the land without a cross word no matter how long or hard the day he'd put in.

Charli. God, Charli.

"Who?" Wade asked, unable to say more.

"Coach Carr had a heart attack a few days ago."

While Wade reeled, Joel continued, his voice somber. Wade heard snatches of what his old friend said—"bypass surgery" and "Lorelie is doing too much"—but the rest couldn't cut through the white noise buzzing in his ears.

Coach getting sick? How was that even possible? He remembered a strapping man with a quick wit who didn't tolerate any crap from his players, especially when they strayed too close to his only child, Lorelie. She was a tomboy who'd been more than capable of taking care of herself, but that hadn't stopped Coach from warning the guys that they better mind their manners in her presence. Since none of the boys had dared date her themselves, they'd formed a sort of black-and-silver Titan shield around her, making it nearly impossible for her to meet anyone new.

Not that there was a whole lot of new in Quinn anyhow. Hadn't that been one of the reasons Wade had used to explain his need to split the minute he had his G.E.D. in hand? He hadn't even been able to tolerate sticking around the last few months until graduation. His future in music couldn't wait.

Neither could his need to get away from the sight of Colt and Charlene together. Laughing. Dancing. Kissing.

More. So much more.

Now Coach was in the hospital. Recuperating from the sounds of things, at least. Still, how was he even supposed to unglue his vocal cords enough to reply? Shock had frozen them in place.

"Hey man, you still there?"

"Yeah. I'm here. Look, what do you need me to do?" Now that he'd figured out how to speak again, the words flooded out of his mouth. "I'm sure there are expenses not covered by insurance. I can send—"

"We need you," Joel interrupted quietly. "Not your money, just you."

Wade fell silent.

"I know you have a tight schedule, and you can't just pick up and leave Nashville."

Oh yes, I can. I need to. "I'll head back as soon as I can," Wade said before sense kicked in and demanded he make the same excuses he'd made to his family over and over again about visiting Quinn. He wasn't still avoiding his hometown after all these years. And Colt.

And Colt's wife.

Ex-wife now. Still fucking hurt. He figured it always would, like that old kicking injury that ached every time it rained. Just one look into Charlene's dark brown eyes would bring it flaring back to life.

"Great." Joel exhaled. "It's going to be so good to have you back home again."

Wade tipped back his mirrored sunglasses and faced his tired blue eyes in the rearview mirror. Home was a nice word.

Too bad he wasn't sure he had one to go back to.

CHAPTER ONE

"You going to help me get this feed up on the shelf or just stare at it?"

Charlene Martinez braced her hands on her hips and eyed the shelf above her head. "You do realize that I'm not even tall enough to reach that shelf, never mind haul a fifty-pound bag of cornmeal up on it, right?"

"Mind over matter, sister friend. Isn't that part of that yoga lifestyle you preach?" With a sassy grin, Paige smacked Charlene on the ass and proceeded to haul the bag of feed up on the shelf by herself without even breaking a sweat. Her voluptuous curves damn near popped out of her tight top, but Paige never noticed the admiring glances from the ranchers and cowboys circling the store. She never would've believed the men frequented Wilcox's Grub and Grain as much for a glimpse of her as to take advantage of the best feed prices in all of Quinn.

Charlene glanced down at her own pathetically flat chest. The truth was that her best friend had a frigging hot rack, better than the thirteen-point buck on the wall above the cash register.

"There. Took care of that. I swear, Mr. Mondell always calls up with the craziest orders. Today it was six bags of the—" Paige stopped and turned, pursing her lips. "Okay, go ahead. Slap me in the mouth a few times until my brain kicks in."

Charlene had to laugh. She hadn't even gotten the significance of the name Paige had mentioned until her brain connected the rest of the dots. Mr. Mondell meant Drake Mondell, also known as one half owner of C&D Horse Training. The C referred to Colt Bennett.

Her ex-husband. Three years' ex, as a matter of fact, though everyone in town gave her sympathetic looks whenever Colt was brought up, as if he'd dumped her high and dry and bedded a dozen fillies since.

So he'd sort of dumped her. But that was only because she'd hung on way too long to something she should've let go of years before.

Live and learn, her abuelita always said. Charlene was fixing to get that tattooed on her ass, because it stuck out so far that she was sure to see it whenever she got the yen to do naked yoga at home.

"Nothing to worry about. Drake's a friend of mine, just as he is yours. Besides, you know me and Colt are amicable," Charlene said, patting Paige on the back as she hustled behind the counter to check inventory.

Colt and Drake weren't the only best friends who'd gone into business together. Three years ago, Paige had inherited Wilcox's from her grandfather upon his passing and she hadn't been ready to let it go. She also hadn't been willing to take over running the feed store herself. Since Charlene had just gotten out of her marriage—*extremely* amicable, thank you very much, which probably spoke to the lack of passion she and Colt had endured for the bulk of their relationship—she'd been at loose ends. Along with helping out at Rosa's, her mama's Mexican restaurant, Charlene also taught a couple of yoga classes a week and hoped to maybe one day open her own studio. The college courses she'd taken while helping out on the Bennett farm hadn't given her quite enough background to feel comfortable managing her own business yet.

She'd ended up *sharing* a business instead.

Three years later, she and Paige were partners, the feed store was turning a tidy profit and she was sexy, single and free. Hell, two out of three wasn't bad. At least her yoga classes kept her flexible for all the sex she wasn't having. But that might change someday. A girl could dream, right?

Paige made a noise in her throat. "I do know that, but it's just not natural to get on that well with an ex. I mean, y'all could grab a pizza together and not even give each other the side eye. That's just flat-out wrong."

Laughing, Charlene hopped up on the stool behind the counter and crossed her legs before pulling her clipboard onto her lap. "What's wrong with it? I've known Colt since high school."

And Colt's little sister, Hollie. And Wade.

Thinking about him made her nervous for more reason than one. Her whole family was heavily superstitious, avoiding black cats and not stepping under ladders, and she half suspected musing about Wade might make him appear.

Besides, thoughts of Wade led to thoughts of Wade's eyes, that faded denim blue that crackled to life as easily as his sexy songs crackled through her radio. Wade's lips, crooked and oh-so-soft. And Wade's hands, broad with blunt-tipped fingers that had cradled her cheeks so tenderly the one and only time they'd kissed.

"You're divorced. That means you're supposed to hate each other's—well, hello there. Speak of the very fine devil." Paige's voice took on that honeyed quality she adopted as easily as the slight twang she'd developed after moving to the area years ago from New York. Paige might've been born a Yankee, but it was impossible to tell when she didn't want that fact known. "Whatcha doin' over here this time of day, Mr. Bennett? Your partner already called in an order."

"Paige, you've known me what, six years now? I think we can dispense with the *Mr.* stuff." Colt turned his easy grin on Charlene. Only someone who knew him as well as she did would be able to discern the tension around his eyes and mouth. "You had lunch yet?"

Charlene sat up straighter and tried to mentally scrub the Wade-induced flush from her cheeks. Especially when she was face-to-face with his older brother. It wasn't a new predicament to find herself in, but the whole brother-vs-brother thing in her head was getting old. Not that there had ever been any real contest. Colt had first been her boyfriend, then a few years after high school, the man who had offered her forever.

Wade had just kissed her to satisfy some competition thing he'd had going with Colt—or heck, maybe he'd lost a bet—before he left town for good.

Whatever Wade's reasons, that momentary lapse in judgment on her part had caused her a whole lot of trouble over the years. Never mind the fantasies of going further than kissing instigated by that one stolen moment. Her future mother-in-law had witnessed the tail end of it, and had perennially doubted Charlene throughout the length of her marriage to her eldest son. She and Wade had never been alone for more than a few minutes for the five years she and Colt had been married, but it hadn't mattered. The die was cast. She was the scarlet woman, minus the A on her chest.

Amazing what repercussions a dumbass move at seventeen could have on someone's entire life.

She cleared her throat and refocused on Colt's face. "No. I haven't. You got something cooking?" He had to, because as friendly as they were, they usually didn't have impromptu lunch dates.

Something was up. If the way he kept cracking his jaw meant anything, it was something big.

"Sure do. I'm craving some of your mama's fajitas something fierce." Colt slid his grin Paige's way. "Hey, why don't you join us?"

The out-of-left-field invitation to Paige seemed to knock Colt off his stride as much as it did Paige. They were all friends, and friends ate lunch together, but Colt's stiff-shouldered appearance suggested more was at work here than the simple sharing of a meal.

"It's the middle of the day, Mr. Bennett."

"Call me Colt, all right?" His good-natured smile was fading fast. "Come on, can't you two take a break? Maybe let Steve the stockboy run the register for an hour?"

"His name is just Steve, not Steve the stockboy, and he does many other vital tasks 'round here." Paige rolled her eyes and elbowed Charlene. "Go on and get this guy out of here, would you? Some of us can't take off for long lunches and margies."

Colt crossed his arms over his massive chest. "Yeah, and that someone isn't you, since you're the boss and can do whatever you damn well please."

Paige's golden brown eyes flashed with a rare show of temper. "Maybe that's how you run your business, but it's not how I run mine." With a swish of her hips, she headed into the back room. Then she leaned out and called to Charlene, "See? *Flat-out wrong.*"

"What's her problem?" Colt leaned an arm on the counter. "I just wanted to take you ladies to lunch."

"I think she's sick of Mexican food or something." Shaking her head, Charlene sighed and set aside her clipboard.

Unless Charlene was very mistaken, she was pretty sure her best friend resented Colt's seemingly easygoing approach toward work. Paige had scrabbled for every nickel since she was a kid raised by a single mother. While Colt hadn't been born with a silver spoon either, he'd always given off an air of indulgence that transcended his bank balance. Both before and after his brief stint in the NFL, he'd acted as if he never worried about money. Though he now spent long hours getting dirty working with his horses, he still retained the bearing of a casually rich man who rarely lifted a finger.

Still, it was odd for Paige to get irritated so easily. Normally she had a sunny disposition that alternately made Charlene envious or annoyed, depending on Charlene's own level of caffeine imbalance that day.

15

"What about you?" Colt asked. "Are you off Mexican too or can we go get some lunch?"

Taking off for lunch would mean long hours tonight on inventory after the yoga class she was scheduled to teach. She'd hoped to maybe head down to the lake to cool off. A midnight swim sounded fun. Perhaps her friends Lela or Annabelle—AJ now—would be up for a dip too. Late June in Texas meant lots of cutoffs and low-cut tops and swimming whenever possible.

But hell, now she was starving. She'd just have to swim tomorrow.

"I'm never going to be off Mexican, Colton. One hundred percent born and bred, remember?" Offering him a grin to break the tension caused by Paige's abrupt exit, she bent to grab her purse. "I'm up for some of mama's chimichangas. Oh, and ooh, deep fried ice cream. Screw my diet."

Colt grinned and passed a hand over his closely-shorn dark hair. "Now you're talking. It's probably better Paige didn't come anyway."

She was tempted to ask why, then decided she didn't want to risk ruining her digestion. Angst never went well with her mama's cooking.

Half an hour later, they faced each other across one of the brightly-patterned tablecloths in her mama's restaurant and scarfed down fajitas and chimichangas while they regaled each other with tales from work. They didn't see each other that often anymore, maybe once or twice a month, but they always slipped into conversation without trouble. But today Colt clearly had something on his mind beyond the youngest Daly girl's riding lessons, though he wouldn't spit it out no matter how much she poked and prodded.

Then a disturbing thought occurred to her. "Is it Coach?"

Colt blinked his unnaturally long dark lashes. "Is Coach what?"

"He's okay, right?"

"Aside from having a serious heart attack and bypass surgery? Uh yeah."

She blew out a breath. "That's not what I meant. I know all that. Did something new happen? Is his rehabilitation not going well?"

"Why would you think that?"

"Because you're acting weird."

Colt's tightened lips smoothed out into a facsimile of a smile. "Am I now?" He leaned back in the booth. "Here I thought we were having a pleasant lunch."

"We are, but something's up with you. You should just tell me what and not make me guess."

"Can't a guy just want to have lunch with a woman he cares about?"

Charlene rolled her eyes, unable to believe she'd ever fallen for that charm he put on as easily as he tugged on his khakis. Not that it wasn't very effective, but it was also transparent as hell when you knew where to look. "I'm your ex-wife. We're not just buddies."

"No. You're right. Which is why I—" Colt broke off as her cell buzzed with an incoming text. "Go ahead and get that."

"I'll be just a second," she said.

As soon as she glimpsed the message from her friend Lela, she realized why Colt was acting so damn fidgety.

"I'm down at Sally's for lunch and just heard a rumor that Wade's back in town. Wanted to give you a heads-up if you don't already know. Do you know? If so, why didn't you tell me?"

Charlene smiled in spite of the hummingbirds fluttering to life inside her belly. Yet again her superstitious nature had been proved right. She'd been on edge, worrying that even thinking of Wade might conjure his presence, and he'd already been back in Quinn.

And Colt had danced around the subject without saying a damn thing.

Gritting her teeth, Charlene typed a response. "First I'm hearing about it. But I'll get the scoop and clue you in ASAP."

"You better. Think we'll need Ben & Jerry's tonight?" Before Charlene could respond, Lela sent another text. "Never mind. I need to refresh my supply anyway."

Charlene suppressed a sympathetic smile. With Lela's ex-boyfriend, Tucker, and the rest of the guys from the high school championship team back in town due to Coach's heart attack, Lela was revisiting her own high school heartbreak.

Difference was Charlene had no intention of spending any more time with Wade than necessary. She'd untangled herself from the Bennett boys years ago, and she wasn't about to climb astride that prickly haystack one more time.

Charlene sent back another quick text. "Okay, sounds good. Talk to you later. Oh, and don't forget the Chunky Monkey." She set aside her phone and reached for her lemonade. A long sip later, she wasn't any closer to knowing how to broach the subject with Colt.

It wasn't a thing. It honestly wasn't. So she'd kissed Wade. Or he'd kissed her. Big whoop. It had happened over twelve years ago. Ancient, forgettable history.

So why was her heart thudding in her ears like she'd just finished an incline workout on the treadmill?

"All right, I'm done stalling." Colt pushed aside his demolished plate of fajitas and braced his massive forearms on the table. He still had his linebacker's physique, that was for sure. "My brother's headed back to see Coach."

She nodded, her reply turning to dust that clogged her throat. *His brother.* Which meant this held much more significance for him than it did for her. She cared about

Wade—he'd been her brother-in-law for five years, after all, and her own brother Rafe's best friend for years before that—but his arrival in town affected Colt so much more.

And this bystander would just stay safely on the sidewalk until the Wade Parade finished passing through town.

"Uh, how do you feel about that?"

"How should I feel?" He leaned back and shoved a hand through his hair. "I've barely seen the guy in the past decade. We hardly even talk at Christmas. Hell, I got a fucking divorce, and he didn't even send as much as an 'I'm sorry' but here he is, running back for Coach." Before she could reply, he held up a hand. "I know that was a dick thing to say."

"Yeah, kinda. A divorce isn't a death."

"Tell that to my lawyer." Though he said it with a cheeky grin, she didn't find it particularly amusing. Especially since she'd asked for a paltry amount of alimony in spite of her own attorney advising her to demand much more. She'd certainly had a case, since she'd put in so many hours on the Bennett farm. But all she'd wanted was to be done.

Now it felt like she was being sucked back into Bennett drama, and she'd forgotten her hip waders.

"Sorry," he said, heaving out a breath. "You know I don't mean that."

"I don't know what you mean. I also don't know what you expect me to say about Wade. I'm happy he's coming back," she hastened to add. "I'm glad for you and your folks and Hollie, and especially for Coach. They were close. I think it'll do him some good to have all the old team reunited."

"Yeah. You're right. It will. My parents are overjoyed. He called them and Hollie to let them know he was on his way." Colt's gaze drifted above her head to the framed photos on the wall of her mama's favorite singers. She had eclectic taste, so they ranged from José José to Elvis. "You think Rosa will put Wade's picture up here someday?"

She didn't know why it made her laugh—or why the sound caught in her chest, like a breath she couldn't fully take. "I'm not sure she's ever even heard his music."

"Sure she has," he said easily. "We used to talk about him. She asked me once if he would come play a set here sometime." He looked down at his hands. "I had to tell her he rarely returned my calls, so I couldn't call and ask."

"Colt," she began, but he didn't let her finish.

"You have to help me," he said, leaning forward.

"Me?" She sprung backwards, pressing her spine to the back of the booth as if she could evade the urgency in his expression. "How can I help you?"

Surely he didn't want her to intercede on his behalf with his brother. If so, how awkward would that be? She had never told him about the kiss, but she'd always assumed he knew. His mother certainly hadn't been shy about making insinuations that she'd tell Colt what had happened the second Charlene stepped out of line. But perhaps she never had.

Or maybe he simply didn't think it mattered anymore. *Ancient history, remember?*

Cripes, she was acting like a junior high girl instead of a divorced woman of the world. Wade had probably kissed hundreds—maybe thousands—of women in the interim since their all-too-brief lip lock. Women trembled at the sound of his voice and tossed lacy underthings on the stage when he crooned. She was nothing to him. Less than nothing.

A memory. A mistake. A girl he'd forgotten.

"I think he resented me going into the NFL. I don't know, maybe he thought he should've had a shot." Colt sighed. "That if I hadn't been there taking the glory, there would've been more room for him."

Of course. *She* wasn't even a factor. Not that she truly believed she could've come between the two men for even a second, but sometimes her thoughts turned fanciful and she imagined that maybe Wade had avoided Quinn because of *her*. Perhaps seeing her hurt, just a little. They'd come so close to having a chance at something, back when it had seemed like everything she wanted was in reach. Even if it meant risking it all.

Charlene swallowed and toyed with the napkin on her lap. After her papa's early death, her mama had warned her to stay away from dreamers like Wade, because they'd never be able to take care of her and her future kids. She needed someone she could count on to be a stable provider, like Colt.

Colt, who'd aimed toward professional football from the time he was a kid.

Colt, who had divorced her when he'd realized what she had known for too long—any spark between them had vanished after she'd miscarried the baby that had led to their shotgun wedding. Besides, she didn't need anyone to provide for her. She was doing just fine on her own.

But if Wade had ever truly looked her way, she wouldn't have cared about her mama's admonition. She would've climbed on the back of his beat-up Harley and ridden off into that dust-encrusted sunset with him, because she could see the future in his eyes.

Or she had, once. So long ago. Back when possibilities had stretched in front of her like a ribbon, and she couldn't make the spool unfurl fast enough.

"You think he hasn't been around home much for over a decade because he resented your success in the NFL? He's had some success of his own, you know."

"I do know, and I'm happy for him. There's something, Char. Don't know what, but we used to be close. You used to be close to him too."

Yep, there went that dusty sensation in her throat. Any minute she'd start choking. "He was Rafe's friend first."

Rafe hadn't done much better than she had after Wade had left town with his G.E.D. and a fistful of ambition, set on chasing fame and fortune. For two kids who hadn't lived in Quinn long, Wade had been a lifeline. They'd lost their father shortly before moving, and then they'd lost their first real friend.

Of course she'd still had Colt and her other friends on the cheerleading squad, but Wade's absence had created a hole for her and Rafe. Not to mention Wade's little sister Hollie, who idolized her big brother and collected every news clipping about him. And apparently Colt had dealt with a hole of his own as well.

"He was your friend too," Colt insisted. "You had a bond, something special."

"Not that special or he wouldn't have left town without warning," she snapped, almost as surprised as Colt seemed to be about the bitterness in her tone.

"I think he needed to go more than he needed to stay. That wasn't about us."

"How do you know that, since you don't know why he's stayed gone?"

Colt tipped back his head to stare at the bright orange ceiling. Minute stress fractures marred the paint. Her mama adored Rosa's and worked her fingers to the bone—today was the first day she'd taken off in weeks, and that was only because she'd finally hired a new manager—but there was no denying the restaurant had seen better days. It needed a couple of coats of paint, maybe some new tablecloths and chairs.

Charlene fiddled with her napkin. Helping her mother gather the funds to spiff up the restaurant was what she needed to focus on, not Wade Bennett. That ship had sailed so long ago that she barely even remembered when he'd claimed space at her dock.

"I don't know," he said finally. "I'm grasping at straws, because it comes down to one thing. I miss my brother. Plain and simple." He lowered his head and met her gaze. "I need your help. I wouldn't ask if it wasn't important, Char. You know that."

She did know that, and it was the one reason she hadn't thrown down her napkin and charged out of there before she said yes. It should be simple to meet with Wade and try to help facilitate a little brother bonding. They'd chitchat, relive old times, and then she would suggest Wade and Colt do something fun together, like go bowling. That was a brotherly activity. Heck, maybe Rafe could go too, because he spent way too much time sequestered in his office at his architectural firm. Once Wade agreed, she could extricate herself from the scenario entirely.

No muss, no fuss.

Except her stomach felt like it was being twisted between two fists. And she couldn't imagine anything easy about staring into Wade's summer blue eyes and pretending she hadn't bought every one of his albums or memorized most of his songs. Lying in her bed at night, she let his music surround her, wrapping her in the whiskey-soaked warmth that belonged solely to Wade Bennett's gravelly, heartbroken voice.

God, she was so frigging screwed.

"Okay," she said before she could change her mind.

Colt's brows lifted and his face cleared, as if she'd taken a great weight from his shoulders. "You'll do it?"

"Yes. I'll find out his number and see if he's willing to meet with me. No guarantees," she warned.

"No guarantees. Thank you. This means so much to me."

She gave her ex the brightest smile she could muster. "We'll make this work for everyone. The important thing is Coach, and for Wade to realize how much he was missed."

"Yes. You're right." Colt glanced at his watch. "I better get back to the ranch. You okay to get back to the store?"

"Sure." She gestured to her glass. "I have my lemonade to finish."

"Great. Thanks again. And tell Paige I'm sorry."

"For what?"

Colt grinned as he pulled a handful of bills out of his wallet and tossed them on the table for the check. "Hell if I know. But say I'm sorry anyway."

"Sure." She gave Colt a weak smile and waved as he headed out.

She sat there a few minutes longer, debating her next move. She really needed to get back to work. But she'd also agreed to contact Wade, though she'd forgotten to get the phone number from Colt and Wade probably wasn't listed on Google, considering his celebrity status and all. Calling Hollie or Wade's parents for the number was out. She refused to let them know she was eager to contact Wade again, even if it was at Colt's behest. Talk about irony.

There was one other option she could try. A long shot at best.

She dug out the card she'd tucked in her wallet two Christmases ago. She'd been shocked as hell to get that simple card in her mailbox. Just a scrawled signature at the bottom with a note—*if you want to talk, call me.*

After she'd regained her equilibrium, she'd torn off the number and shoved it in her purse. Otherwise she would've stared at that card for days. Instead she'd hidden it in a pocket and never removed it again until now.

He'd probably changed the number. But what did she have to lose?

Everything.

Two minutes later, she listened to his voice mail and tried not to shiver at the rough timbre of his voice. It wasn't

24

right that he sounded that good. That was just his speaking voice, for pete's sake. But then came the beep and she tried to seem cool. They should get together while he was in town and talk. That would be a good idea. By the time she hung up, the waitress had arrived to clear the table and collect the check.

Which meant it was time to get back to work.

Throughout the rest of her day bustling around at the store and later, teaching her yoga class, she mentally replayed the message she'd left for Wade. She'd probably sounded stupid. Her voice tended to get breathy when she was nervous. For all she knew, he might think she was trying to pick up the big singing star before he was accosted by all the locals.

Unless he already had been. He could be in town this very second. She hadn't pumped Lela for more gossip yet. She also hadn't heard back from Wade.

After class, she'd call her friends and see if they could get together for a late night drink at Pitchers. It was a Thursday, but Lela and AJ both worked for the school district so they were off for the summer. Paige, on the other hand, would've hit the sheets with her eye mask and earplugs at eight on the dot. Early to rise and all that.

As she led the class through the downward dog position, Charlene sent up a quick mental prayer that she would get through the rest of the evening without tripping or falling on her ass.

She managed the latter without trouble. But when she walked out the back door of the studio at a little after nine p.m. and turned to hurry across the parking lot to her car, she caught the tip of her shoe on a groove in the sidewalk and went hurtling into a pair of strong, steady arms that folded her into an equally strong chest.

"What the—who?" She glanced up at the man holding her. There was no doubt he was male, thanks to the smoky citrus scent wrapped around him. And the muscular arms. Mustn't forget the arms.

But when she glimpsed the dark cowboy hat casting the stranger's face in shadow, she knew. Oh, she knew.

"Wade," she whispered.

CHAPTER TWO

She was even tinier than Wade remembered.

Charlene Carmen Martinez had always been a little thing. Her brother Rafe—older by eleven months and about twice her size—might've been her twin in coloring if not demeanor. They both shared the same midnight dark hair and gleaming brown eyes surrounded by thick black lashes that dusted their cheeks. Not that Wade had made a habit of studying his buddy's lashes, but he'd heard enough wistful comments among the girls at school.

And he *had* spent a lot of time studying Charlene.

Now she was squirming away from him, her breaths coming fast as she sputtered and tried to put distance between them. More distance. As if they hadn't already suffered through more than a decade's worth.

At least *he'd* suffered. Jury was out on her.

"Hey there, darlin'. Sorry to startle you but you would've hit the ground if I hadn't snatched you up."

"Startled?" She tugged at the thin T-shirt she wore with the miniscule pair of shorts that served as her workout clothes. He'd watched her instruct her class through the window for a few minutes, until he'd grown too uncomfortable— particularly down south—and needed to pace off his frustration. "I'm just on the verge of having a heart attack is all."

He didn't mean to laugh, but man, it felt good when she joined him, that musical chuckle of hers mixing with his until they smoothed out into a beautiful melody. Once it tapered off, she stared up at him with her big eyes and pursed her unglossed lips. "You didn't call me back."

"Sorry about that. I was still on the road." Christ, he'd apologized to her twice in under two minutes. That was enough of that. She should be apologizing to him for causing him to compare every other woman to her since he was a teenager.

Worst of all? None of them ever measured up.

"You drove here?" Surprise rang in her voice. "Yourself? What about your limo? Or your jet?"

He nearly laughed again until he realized she was serious. Yes, he'd done well for himself, and he wouldn't have to worry about getting a job outside of music for quite some time, even if everything fell apart tomorrow. That didn't mean he had a limo or a Lear jet at the ready. He gave too much of his money away for one thing, funneling it into programs for underprivileged youth and to keep music in schools.

For another, Wade Bennett wasn't the big commodity he'd once been. He wasn't exactly tucking his tail between his legs on his return trip home, but there were reasons that his record company was sending some hotshot rhythm guitarist/songwriter to meet with him while he was in Quinn. The guy was based in LA, but apparently making the trip out to Texas was worth his while. Or so Wade's management team thought. Wade wasn't certain of anything yet, but at least two of his buddies from his backing band, Glen and Jared, would be in town for the meeting with this Gray Duffy dude. Wade had insisted on it.

He needed somebody on his side when he was dealing with people who wanted to change his music. Change *him*, when it came right down to it.

And now there was Charli, looking up at him as if he was some major superstar, commanding jets and stretch limos and filling up stadiums. The reality was much less dazzling.

"I drove my pickup." He'd dealt with the disappointment from fans and well-meaning friends when they discovered he didn't wallpaper his walls with money. People enjoyed harboring their delusions about those in the music business, and sometimes the truth stung more for them than the guy signing the checks. "My truck is six years old and has over eighty thousand miles on it. It's not top-of-the-line. In fact, my passenger seatbelt has been problematic for two months."

She frowned. "You must not have passengers all that often."

"Nope, usually just Melody. My dog."

"Oh. What happened to Countess?"

"She passed about five years after I got to Nashville. A year after that, I got Melody when she was just a pup." He smoothed Charlene's T-shirt sleeve down without thinking and had to smother a groan at the dampness of the fabric. She'd sweated damn near through it. So if he looked to the left and downward a bit, he'd get to see her small, perfect breasts outlined in snug white cotton that molded to every swell and dip.

Not looking.

"Aww, I'm sorry to hear that. Countess was a sweetheart. I bet Melody is too. Where is she right now? Back home in Nashville?"

Nashville would never be home, but she didn't need to know that. He had a role to play while he was in town—the swaggering, successful singer—and he'd fulfill his part. "No, she's with me. I rented a place while I'm in town. You remember the old Sutter place on Casper Lake?"

"Yeah, I do. That's right near Lela's house actually. You're renting it?"

He pushed a hand in the back pocket of his jeans. He hadn't realized Lela was so close by to where he was staying. She was a great person, like most of the old crew he'd run with in high school. But her proximity meant the rest of his old friends would be nearby too. They'd all been thick as thieves, and where Lela was, Randi, Joel, Carter and the rest were sure to follow.

And that rest included his brother.

"How come you're not staying out at your family's ranch? There's plenty of room. Unless you don't think the accommodations will be up to snuff."

It took him a minute to realize she was teasing. He wiped a hand over the sweat accumulating on the back of his neck and let out a soft chuckle. "Of course they are. You know how much I love that place. I just thought I'd give them all some privacy. Heard Colt's staying there now too," he added, waiting for her to confirm or deny that his brother had moved into one of the outbuildings on their family's property after his divorce.

Instead she cocked her head. "I didn't realize the Sutter place was being rented out now. I thought they were in the market for a buyer."

"They probably were, but the real estate game in town's not what it once was. Or so I was told when I booked the place for the two weeks I'll be in town."

"Two weeks?" she burst out. "That's all?" Then she cleared her throat and played with the strap of her purse, managing to pull her shirt up enough to catch the fabric on her nipples.

Her *hard* nipples. God, he needed to keep his gaze above her nose.

"I mean, I just figured you'd be in town longer since you haven't seen your folks or...Colt in so long." She canted her head and the light coming from the studio glimmered on her dangling gold earrings. She'd always worn sexy earrings, the kind that were so long they nearly touched her shoulders. Nice to see some things hadn't changed.

And while he was admiring her jewelry, she was still talking about his brother.

"He'd like to see you, you know. I think he misses you. No, I know he misses you. You guys used to be so close—"

"Come back with me to the Sutton place," he said suddenly, as surprised to be making the request as she seemed to be to hear it. "We have some unfinished business, don't you think?"

It took everything he possessed not to mention the kiss he'd laid on her the day he left. Seeing her after all this time brought the memory roaring back with a vengeance.

All of the memories. How could it have been twelve years since he'd lived in this town?

She grew too still. "Do we?"

"To my mind we do. And you can meet Melody. You mentioned wanting to get together." *Tell me it wasn't just to talk about Colt.*

Her ex-husband. Couldn't forget that part.

Even in the dim light, he could make out her throat working and the way her fingers fluttered over the hem of her shirt. Did she know he couldn't stop checking out her breasts? He hoped not. They'd always been friends, and for five years, she'd been his sister-in-law. Plus, he was now just a stranger in this town, visiting on a pass that would expire all too soon. He had no right to look at her any other way than respectfully.

Wanting to fuck her up against the brick wall of the studio was definitely *not* kosher.

"I'm supposed to meet the girls," she began, but then she shook her head. "No, they'll understand. It's not like I don't see them all the time. You're only here for a little while. God, Wade, it's been too long."

Before he could prepare, she launched herself at him and dug her fingers into his biceps, holding on with a strength he never would've guessed she possessed. "Don't you dare stay out of contact so long again," she said in a fierce undertone, her words piercing through the cotton of his shirt and burrowing into his chest. His heart. "You have friends and family who love you in this town, and we won't allow you to forget us. No matter how big your britches get, you still need those who helped you put them on in the first place."

He laughed. Simply couldn't help it. He also couldn't help leaning down to sniff her hair, only to discover it smelled like peaches. But not the wholesome kind. These had been drenched in brandy, making her scent that much darker and more intoxicating.

Though he hadn't had a drop to drink in months, he had a feeling he wouldn't be able to stop himself from indulging in a much more dangerous addiction tonight.

He slid his hand up her back and registered the quiver that chased his touch up her spine. It was easy, too easy, to grab a fistful of her long, wavy dark hair to tug her head back, so he could make sure her gaze rested on his face when he tested the waters. "You start talking about britches, sweetheart, and you'll make a man think you're looking to lose yours."

Her eyebrows shot up and for a second, he wondered if he'd gone straight from testing the waters to boiling frogs. A line that might work on a woman in Nashville wasn't going to cut it with a girl who'd known him since he'd had that stupid cowlick that wouldn't stay flat no matter how many times he combed it down. He was being stupid if he thought he could seduce—

"What makes you think I'm wearing any?"

He swallowed and shifted back just far enough that she wouldn't be able to feel the column of steel in his jeans. She wasn't deterred. She only took another step forward and fit herself against him fully, the corner of her mouth lifting as she discovered what he'd never be able to hide.

Had never *been* able to hide, since the day she'd marched into Mr. Donnelly's ninth grade math class and claimed the first seat in the first row. School had been important to her, and she'd refused to settle for slouching in the back row when she could be right up front.

Wade had skipped second grade himself, which accounted for why he'd been in the same class as his brother, but that had been aptitude more than application. By high school, he'd skipped hitting the books for long hours practicing his guitar. But not Charlene. She'd never backed down from a challenge when it came to her studies, and apparently she didn't in her personal life either. Even a half-assed, half-thought-out one like Wade's.

At his silence, she moved even closer. "You want me?" she asked softly.

It was the question mark at the end that undid him. The bravado he'd shrugged on fell away, leaving only raw, honest need behind.

He dragged her up on her tiptoes so that they lined up better. "I always have."

She shuddered and curled against him, her heartbeat a heavy thud against his that reverberated all the way down his spine. "Fine time for you to tell me that, Bennett."

That name—the one that was his, and had once been hers—should've doused cold water on his libido. Doing this was crazy. Fuck, he'd only been in the city limits for what, two hours? Just long enough to drive by Coach's to find out he was already in bed. Wade intended to return first thing tomorrow, though he suspected talking to Coach wouldn't be a walk around the corral. Days of reckoning came eventually, and deliverance wasn't always issued through force.

Sometimes it was the quiet words that struck deepest.

Like Charli's breathless question, still echoing in his head like a song stuck on repeat. *"You want me?"*

Yes, yes, fuck yes.

"You're right," he said, equally soft. His thumb brushed her lower lip and she trembled before her teeth scraped over his flesh, offering the slightest hint of pain. He sucked in a breath and realized he'd need an oxygen tank before this night was through. "Maybe it's time I start showing you."

She nodded and met his gaze, her chin coming up with the defiance he'd always loved most about her. She was the strongest, most stubborn girl—now woman—he'd ever met. "Past time, don't you think?"

"Yes." He debated lowering his mouth to hers and decided if he started kissing her, he wouldn't be able to stop without taking her up against the building. That wouldn't do, even if he was craving a sample of what he'd secretly always thought should've been his. She had the right to decide for herself which brother she preferred, but Colt hadn't wanted her like he had. How could he, when even all these years later, that want jutted up inside him, demanding to be acknowledged? "Come home with me," he gritted out.

"Wade. We should talk." It wasn't reproach in her voice, but something else. That last bit of reluctance before longing eroded it.

Or that could be just wishful thinking on his part.

"We will." He withdrew his thumb from between her plump lips. "After."

That right there was where the rubber met the road. He'd never expected for his first conversation with her after all this time to take this kind of tone, but he'd underestimated the need inside him. Need unleashed by one look into warm, wanton brown eyes that were full of missing him.

He'd been responsible for too damn long, and all it had gotten him was a life alone, other than those rare nights with women he met on tour. They represented brief snatches of pleasure that were like the taste of candy on the tongue—fleeting and incapable of satisfying true hunger.

Licorice never made a good substitute for brandied peaches.

"Okay. Let's do this." She stepped back and took a few definitive steps toward the parking lot. A few scattered vehicles still remained. "Uh, which truck is yours?"

He cupped her shoulders, guiding her forward. "The black Silverado."

"Black seems to be a theme with you." She nodded at his cowboy hat. "Are your boxers black too?"

"You'll find out soon enough." When she braced, he curled his fingers around the tops of her arms. "Just a turn of phrase. You don't have to find out anything. I don't expect—"

"Don't overanalyze it. In fact, don't say anything at all." She shrugged him off and strode ahead, her purposeful stride not doing a dang thing to diminish the sway of her hips. "I want to just…do it."

He couldn't hold back his chuckle as he pushed the button on his key fob to unlock his truck. "You didn't even buy me dinner first."

She shot him a glance he just knew would be full of fire if he could see her face more clearly. "Forget food, I'm riding a yoga high." Surprising the hell out of him, she turned and grabbed the front of his T-shirt in her fists. "You might want to take advantage of that, Strings."

A grin broke across his face. "I haven't heard that nickname in twelve years. I missed it."

"About the same amount of time since I've thought of it." She frowned and turned away, opening her door before he could. She boosted herself up and disappeared into the darkened cabin, leaving him to blow out a breath before he rounded the hood.

This was either his worst idea ever or his best mistake. There was no way it could be anything but a disaster on some level, because she was his brother's ex. Not just ex.

Ex-wife.

He climbed inside and gripped the wheel, facing straight ahead. Her breathing sounded too fast, about on pace with his. "Look, I know this has to be awkward for you."

"For me? Yeah. For you too. And awkward isn't the word I'd use." She stopped fumbling with the seatbelt to rub his thigh, repeating the same gesture she had when they were in school. Somehow back then it hadn't seemed quite so erotic when her fingers edged along his inner leg, though he'd endured more than a few hard-ons due to her innocent caresses.

But this was frigging incendiary. She was burning him up with only her touch.

He wouldn't look at her. If he didn't look until they crossed the threshold of his rental place, he wouldn't drag her across the console and into his lap. He refused to ruin what might be his only chance with the girl of his dreams.

The girl your brother married.

"Fuck," he muttered, pressing his fist into his forehead. The low throb there echoed the one in his groin. "What word?" he asked a little too desperately. "What word would you use?"

"Overdue," she said, her voice so hushed that he wondered if he'd imagined that she had spoken.

He shut his eyes and tightened his grip on the wheel. "Yes. God, yes. But I don't want you to worry."

"About what?"

Her question barely intruded on the monologue he'd started. "I know that Quinn's a small town, and people talk. Most are well-meaning, yeah, and gossip is usually harmless. This wouldn't be. So I don't want you to be concerned that I'll run my mouth." He opened his eyes to glance at her, despite the pain looking at her caused. She was too beautiful, and he wanted her too much. "What happens between us will stay that way, I promise. No one will ever have to know except you and me."

She stopped toying with the seatbelt—he'd told her it wasn't fully functional, hadn't he?—and let it wind

36

halfheartedly back into the holder. "Oh, is that so?" she asked, her tone cool enough to turn the steam fogging the windows into ice. "Thank you for letting me know the score."

"Score?" He went back to rubbing his forehead. There might actually be a jackhammer in his skull, one that only activated when he traveled into the Quinn city limits. "I'm sorry, I don't know what you mean."

"I'll tell you what I mean, you jackass. You think that just because you hobnob with the rich and famous and have songs on the radio that women are just supposed to spread their legs for you. As long as they don't forget to keep your precious privacy intact. Is that the price of admission?"

His eyebrows lifted. "What the hell are you talking about?"

"Like you don't know." She whacked his arm with her purse and pushed open the door. "Pretending it's all for my own good. *Oh, sure, honey, we'll have a nice time and then you'll never speak my name again.* You know, in case you're like the Candyman and saying your name in the mirror makes you appear. Bastard." She added a few more colorful words in Spanish, ones he was glad he couldn't immediately translate. He doubted they would be flattering.

"I think you've misunderstood me," he said once she paused to take a breath.

"Did you or did you not ask me to be your secret mistress?"

Had he asked her that? It was all so hazy now. Hell, maybe he had.

Maybe he should've gone right to the rental and stayed in for the night, because obviously the long hours of driving had caught up to him and he wasn't fit for human consumption. Deciphering the hieroglyphics that made up the female mind was definitely out until he'd gotten some sleep and a lot more caffeine, in that order.

"I'm not sure," he said finally. "Perhaps that's what you heard, but I'm pretty certain that's not what I intended to say."

The sound she made indicated her opinion on *that.* "Look, I only called you because of Colt. He asked me to try to, I don't know, kind of be a bridge between you—"

A harsh laugh escaped Wade, heralding the swift flare of agony in his chest. It obliterated sense and everything else but the need to strike back like he'd been struck. This was only the latest blow. The first had landed more than twelve years ago. "A bridge. Is that what they're calling it now?"

She turned away from him. For a second, he really believed that would be it. She'd keep walking and his last chance with her would vanish as fast as it had appeared. Then she looked over her shoulder, her face caught in the beam from one of the lights that ringed the lot. All he could see was her eyes, sucking him down like Wiley's Gulch at the edge of his parents' property. Dark, dangerous things lurked in their depths, but God, he wanted to discover what they were.

"I don't know how they do things in Nashville, Strings," she said, her voice heartbreakingly soft. "Here in Quinn, we don't play those kinds of games. If I can't sleep with you at night and walk with you in the sunshine during the day, then I'm not taking that ride." She set her jaw with an audible click. "Now or ever."

Then she did walk away, dark hair swinging, the door thudding shut in her wake.

He sat there for a while, long after she'd gotten into her sedan and driven away. He debated putting on the truck and just letting the music wash over him—other people's music, not his own—but right then, the silence was better. Rolling down the window, he stuck his elbow out into the humid night air and sucked in a greedy gulp. They'd sat in that stifling truck for five minutes without a thought to the insufferable heat—other than the one that burned inside them. Inside *him* anyway.

For her. Always for her. Now he'd driven her away and ruined his chance with her.

But that was just it, wasn't it? This wasn't a real chance. It was just a way to relieve some of the pressure and bandage the wound. It wasn't anything more than a quick roll and *fuck*, that pissed him off. He didn't want to settle for a secretive one-night thing, but he'd never believed he'd have the chance for even that. Not with his brother's wife.

Ex-wife. And man, wouldn't she be pissed to know how often he referred to her that way in his head? It was almost as if his conscience couldn't let him forget. Coveting her was wrong. She'd belonged to Colt, and now she should be off-limits.

Perhaps it was better he'd put his foot in it and chased her away. He'd made his ridiculous suggestion for her rather than him. The last thing he wanted was for her to have to deal with any uncomfortable talk in town or worse, attitude from his brother. He didn't care about his own rep. Hell no. He certainly wouldn't have denied himself the opportunity to walk with her in the sunshine. Dreams that huge were hard to come by.

That probably was a good thing, since they hurt like a bitch once they were gone.

He started his truck and drove back to the Sutter place in silence, unable to stand the idea of music. Normally he couldn't drive fifty yards without it on in the background. Tonight the night sounds were more than enough as he idled at stop signs and fought not to aim the truck back into the center of town where Charlene lived. He'd found out from Joel that she taught yoga classes on Thursday nights, so it had been easy enough to track her down. Easy and a big freaking mistake, obviously.

Let her be.

By the time he dropped into bed, he was ready for some oblivion. Staying awake into the wee hours held no appeal. He'd done that often enough lately while he tried to figure out the new course with his career. For once, he intended to shut it all off, with only the music of the frogs, the lake and the night creatures outside his window to lull him into sleep.

A false paradise, that, because while he spent hours unconscious, he didn't get much rest. His dreams were a fractured, jumbled mess, and he replayed them as he slurped down burnt coffee and drove to Coach's ranch early the next morning. Obviously he'd need to up his workouts while he was in town, because pure exhaustion was the only thing that might knock him out enough not to dream.

And now he had something all new to dread.

He'd gotten a status update from Joel about Coach's condition, so at least he could breathe easier about that. Coach was doing better, though he still grew tired quickly and couldn't handle many of the tasks around the ranch. That's where he, Tucker, Jackson, Carter and Colt and some of the other guys from the old high school football team came into play. Not only were they there to offer encouragement, the plan was for them to take on some of the things that Coach could no longer handle. His daughter Lorelie did a great job at filling in the gaps, but she was only one person and on the verge of running herself ragged.

Hopefully his presence would help and not cause more trouble.

He parked the truck and crossed the lawn to the wide porch. He couldn't resist turning to take in the acres of green and brown, surrounded by white picket fences and dotted with livestock and outbuildings. Familiar and oh so different. He'd spent many happy hours working the land here, using sweat equity to chase away the demons in his head. The ones that had made him feel not quite good enough in his hometown, because he'd always wanted to hold a guitar and not a football. Oh, he'd loved the game, no doubt about it. But his overriding passion had always been music.

And eventually, Charlene. Not that he'd ever told her. Nope, he'd let his brother the football star sail in and whisk her away. Well, not that far. The whisking had been to Sally's diner, where Colt had presented her with his class ring. But Wade had seen the handwriting on the wall and shifted toward getting his G.E.D.—and getting out.

Charli wasn't the only reason he'd left town. He'd wanted to make music. Hell, he'd ached to create a life far from everything he knew. Maybe that had been his youth talking or plain stupidity, because it was damn sure hard to breathe in the fresh air out here and watch the sun trickle through the bright blue sky and not think of everything he'd missed.

Like Coach. And his family. And Charli.

The screen door creaked open. "You coming in or just going to loiter out here?"

He grinned and turned to face Lorelie. She was grinning back, her arms held wide. "If this is the welcome home I'm getting, I'm definitely coming in." He wrapped his arms around her waist and lifted her clear off her feet, making her laugh. "Look at you, Miss Pretty Thang. Went and grew up on me, huh?"

"I kinda had to. You were gone an awful long time."

"I came home now and then."

"But you didn't spend much time seeing your old friends. You buzzed in and out again most times before any of us knew you were here." Her eyebrows knitted together. "Even dad."

"Yeah." Sobering, he set Lorelie on her feet and brushed a wayward strand of hair out of her eyes. Growing up without her mother—who had died having her—and with only Coach to raise her had made her tougher than most, and he could practically feel that strength radiating from her now.

Seeing her again really made this feel like home.

"It's so good to see you. A big singing star and all, right here in Quinn." The teasing glint in her eyes didn't lessen the obvious pride in her voice. "We're all so happy for you. They're always playing your music down at Pitchers, you know."

"Aww, come on now. It's no big deal."

"Oh really? How many famous people you seen 'round here?" She pretended to glance around. "Bessie can sure break wind with the best of them, but that isn't too unusual for a cow."

He laughed and wondered how his chest didn't crack open from the effort. It felt like forever since he'd laughed right down into his gut like that. "Bessie's still around? Tough old coot."

"She's not the only one." Lorelie lowered her voice. "Dad just woke up from a nap. I have to warn you, he's not the way you remember."

Genuine fear constricted Wade's throat. With all of his own drama with Colt and Charli, he'd let himself become distracted from the real reason he'd come home. The one that mattered most. "But he's okay, right? He's going to be okay."

She nodded. "Yes. He's doing so much better already. Having all of you back here helps so much." She punched him lightly in the shoulder. "What took you so long? The other guys got back in town days ago. Even Tucker showed up here yesterday."

Wade felt the faintest flush burning the back of his neck. He didn't want anyone to know he'd struggled to get himself together in those first couple of days after he'd heard the news about Coach. Then it had been a matter of tying up a lot of loose ends with his record company to account for a sudden trip when they'd been expecting him to meet with that hotshot songwriter. That he'd managed to get the songwriter out to Texas had been a stroke of sheer luck.

"Sorry about that. I wanted to give y'all some time to—"

"Forget we were missing and needing you? Fat chance. Get in this house already." She softened the words with a smile and gave him a light push toward the door. "Don't forget to wipe your boots," she chided as he opened the screen door.

"Yes, ma'am." He did as she asked and looked up in time to see Coach shuffle out of the living room. He had an afghan around his shoulders, which he quickly shoved behind his back.

"Oh, it's you," Coach said, fidgeting as if he was hiding a bomb. "I knew I heard voices."

"You sure did. I think Wade here should sing you a song to help with your recovery." When Wade swiped at her hair, Lorelie ducked and hurried down the hall, leaving them alone.

So alone.

Wade cleared his throat and found it did nothing to lessen the emotion making it tight. Coach had a bandage on his forehead and had definitely lost weight, something that was even more striking on his large frame. "Coach. God, it's good to see you. How long has it been?"

"You know damn well how long. It's been twelve years since you darkened my doorstep, boy."

At least his booming voice hadn't changed. But yep, Wade's initial guess was correct. Coach had no intention of making this easy on him. Wade couldn't say he blamed him.

He pushed his hands in the back pockets of his jeans. He'd intended to shake hands with the older man, but from the glower in Coach's eyes, he wasn't entirely sure he'd accept the gesture.

And you're too much of a coward to try.

"My career makes things difficult," he began.

Coach snorted and tossed the afghan onto a chair. "Right. Your career. Because you don't get time off, right? You don't take holidays now and then." He shook his head. "Your parents have missed you. So has your brother. And Rafe and Charlene."

At the mention of Charlene, Wade shifted his gaze away to the mat covered with a line of dirt-encrusted boots. A lot of hard work was done by the people who helped out on this ranch.

He missed hard physical labor. The kind that made him drop into bed exhausted at night, too tired to think. His skin overwarm from the sun and his eyes just bleary enough not to see what he didn't want to.

Too worn out to say words that could hurt others like he hurt. Still.

"Put me to work," he said suddenly. "Whatever needs doing, I'll do it." He stripped off his fancy watch and dropped it without a thought into a bowl of change on the table beside the door. "Coach, please," he said when the other man remained silent.

"You think it's that simple, hmm? Just come back and it'll be like the years apart don't matter?" Coach rubbed his jaw, the tiniest smile creasing his face. "You're damn right. Now get over here and give me a proper hello."

Grinning, Wade stuck out his hand, only to find himself pulled into a surprisingly strong bear hug. It wasn't the same strength as the hugs he'd received in high school, but it was close enough to cause some of the worry he'd harbored to disappear.

"That's better." Coach nudged him back and gripped his shoulder. "I'm damn proud of you, Wade Bennett. You chased your dreams and you caught them."

"Thanks." Wade lowered his head. "Some of them anyway."

"Some of them," Coach agreed, releasing his shoulder. "And I have to say I take some responsibility for that. I was the one who told you to make the hard choices, to go where your heart led you. I just never thought it'd lead you out of Quinn without ever looking back."

"I've looked back."

"You didn't look back when it mattered. Colt was gone three years with the NFL before he came back and married Charlene. Three years they weren't together. And where were you?"

God, leave it to Coach to jump right into the nitty-gritty first thing. So much for the past not mattering anymore. "He dated her first."

"Only because you wouldn't take your head out of your ass long enough to take the risk."

"I knew the situation with her family. Rafe told me all about how Mrs. Martinez drummed it into Charli's head that she needed to find a stable man, the kind she could rely on."

"That's not you?"

Wade locked his fingers behind his neck and tipped back his head. "It doesn't matter now."

"Tell me she's not the first place you went when you hit town."

Wade shut his eyes.

"Yeah. Thought so. Wasn't it Shakespeare who talked about the past being prologue? You know damn well as I do that you need to put a period to that business one way or another while you're in town." When Wade opened his eyes and shot Coach a surprised glance, Coach frowned. "What? I taught English. I know Shakespeare."

Wade laughed. "I've missed you so much. I won't stay gone this long again. That's a promise."

"One I'm going to hold you to." Coach cleared his throat. "Can I give you a piece of advice?"

"Wow, never heard you ask before. Normally it's 'Wade, you listen here'."

"We aren't as familiar as we once were. Give it a day or so and we'll be back to our old way of doing things."

"Okay. Shoot."

"She's divorced now. This time, chase another dream."

Wade had to fight the urge to shove his hands in his pockets again. Instead he met Coach's gaze head-on. "What about Colt?"

"Heads-up, boy. Getting divorced usually means the relationship is over. But you know which relationship isn't? Yours with your brother. Stop ducking away from him and stop dancing around Charlene. Try running *to* rather than away. You know, just for a change of pace." Coach clapped him on the back. "Now let's get some of my Lorelie's amazing lemonade and I'll show you what needs doing. I really appreciate all of you boys returning to help out, though I'm completely capable of doing it myself."

"Oh, I know that."

"Don't patronize me. I could still beat your ass on a dash across that field."

Wade smiled. "Yeah, but I wasn't the fastest on the team."

"You weren't the slowest either, and you got where you needed to go most of the time. Come on. There's work to do."

Wade followed Coach down the hall. No arguments there. He had plenty to do, both on and off the land.

And this time, he'd have to think with his head and not his dick or his mouth.

CHAPTER THREE

Charlene pulled up to Coach's late Saturday afternoon and pulled out the picnic basket she'd made up for Coach and Lorelie. Her plan was to get them out of the house to go have a nice, relaxing dinner somewhere, maybe down by Casper Lake, and while they were gone, she'd freshen up their place. In high school, her mama had started a neighborhood cleaning business to make extra money, and Charlene had helped out when her mama needed it. She could wash windows, dust and mop with the best of 'em.

It wasn't much, but Lorelie was exhausted and doing way too much. This would be a small comfort, Charlene hoped. It also had the added benefit of giving her something to do other than dwell on what people were saying around town about Wade's arrival. Everyone was thrilled to have him visit, understandably, but it was hard to hear all the talk without thinking about their disastrous conversation.

Conversation and near-hookup. So near that she'd been frustrated enough to consider bringing Ol' Faithful, her bright pink vibrator, into the shower with her later that night. She tried not to turn to her BOB more often than necessary. It would be all too easy to decide she didn't need a man as long as she kept batteries fully stocked. Heck, she'd practically reached that conclusion even while depriving herself.

It had been way too long since she'd been on a date, never mind get laid. No wonder she'd thrown herself at Wade like a cat in heat. If it hadn't been so long, she never would've entertained such a crazy idea.

A hookup with her ex-husband's brother. Completely ludicrous.

She wasn't that woman. Dating in a small town was hard enough when everyone felt behooved to comment on

Colt's dates. There had been more than a few. Okay, more than a dozen, probably. Still, she'd be damned if the reverse became true and Colt had to hear about her and Wade.

She slammed the trunk and heaved the picnic basket, making it halfway around the car before she realized Lorelie's vehicle wasn't parked in the driveway. Uh-oh. She should've called and made sure they were home—

"Lookin' for Coach?"

Charlene shaded her eyes and shifted to look up at the porch as the screen door slammed shut. And oh crap, she should not have done that. Did she really need to see Wade Bennett, shirtless and sweaty, standing in a patch of sun, dripping as if he were a living Popsicle?

Damn, she wanted to lick him. A lot.

His hair was wet too. He must've just dunked it in the sink after working in the fields. That explained the beads of water gathering on his shoulders like diamonds. More diamonds sprinkled down his carved chest to the dark treasure trail that crept right into his mine—AKA his low-slung pants. Whoa, what a mine it was. He was either packing a giant piece of coal or else she wasn't the only one dealing from a sudden bolt of inappropriate lust.

God, she was still staring. Could. Not. Stop.

"Charlene?" A hint of amusement entered his voice. "Honey, you look like you need a glass of lemonade. It's mighty hot out here."

"Picnic." She held out her basket with its checkerboard blanket tossed jauntily over the handle. "I wanted Coach and Lorelie to go on one. And you know, leave the house while I cleaned it for them. Not saying it's dirty, I just wanted to help out." She took a breath. "So where are they?"

He laughed and oh sweet hell, she loved that sound. "Come on in and we'll get you that lemonade. That sun's a killer."

Being close to you while you're half-naked will kill me first. But she only smiled and nodded before trotting up the steps as if she wasn't the least bit concerned about spending additional time in his sphere. "You're just not used to it anymore. This isn't all that hot."

"Really?" He glanced down at her, his mouth still quirked. "Then why are you sweating?"

Oh Lord. She dabbed at the cleavage revealed by her yellow-and-white sundress. Not exactly cleaning clothes, granted, but she hadn't been willing to take the chance of encountering Wade while wearing ratty clothes. She'd rather be extra careful while tidying up the ranch. "I did a workout right before coming over here," she lied.

Great. So now he'd think she was a hot mess and had put on the sundress without taking a shower first. She should've just admitted that her admiration of him hadn't just soaked her forehead and her cleavage, but her panties too.

They were definitely the biggest casualty of this war.

"Damn, and I missed it. I sure liked watching you the other night." He leaned in and sniffed her hair. Actually sniffed her like a piece of meat. Which shouldn't have been sexy, but so was. "Still smell like peaches. Is that your shampoo or some girly soap?"

"Neither. It's my liniment."

"Say what?"

She had to laugh. "I get sore muscles from working long hours at the feed store and mama's restaurant. I use the liniment to help with them." She nudged his elbow. "Surely you used liniment when you were on the team to help with aching muscles."

"We didn't call it liniment. And yeah, I've probably heard that term before, now that you mention it. It's just been awhile." He scratched his distractingly bare chest. "Does the yoga help too?"

"Absolutely. I couldn't do everything I do if I didn't practice yoga. Pilates too. They've helped my back immensely—hey, what are you doing?" she asked as he took the picnic basket out of her hands.

"You don't need to be hauling around a big basket like this when I'm standing right here. What's in here?" He flipped open the top. "Ham and Swiss on rye? With mustard? Oh man. I'm starving."

"They're not for you," she said primly. She felt bad about denying the man a sandwich, but she'd only made enough for two, and besides, she was almost certain that offering Wade her deli meat was one step away from offering him everything. Again. And she was still pissed from the last time.

Not pissed enough though, unfortunately, because she couldn't help leaning in and doing a little sniffing of her own. Thankfully, he didn't notice. She swallowed her moan as his scents of soap and clean, healthy sweat mingled into something heady. He smelled like summer. Like hard work on a sunny afternoon followed by hard lovemaking on a moonstruck night.

Or maybe just soap and sweat, but still…*mmm*.

"Coach and Lorelie are gone for the afternoon. They went to see one of Coach's friends in Brawley. Coach said he needed a change of scenery."

"Oh. Well then." She tried to take back the picnic basket, but Wade just moved it farther out of reach. That wouldn't do. She needed to get gone. Being alone with him was a recipe for a whole lot of trouble.

Trouble her body yearned for with a capital T.

"Awfully nice of you to make them a picnic. The rest of it, though…your mama doesn't still have that cleaning business, does she?"

"No. She sold it years ago and made a nice profit, actually. It helped give her enough money to buy her restaurant. Rosa's," she explained.

"That's her? Really? I have to stop down there. I've tried a few places since I've been back, but man, nothing has hit the spot like your mother's chiles rellenos used to." He peeked into the basket again. "These sandwiches might tide me over."

She tried not to smile. "I should leave them for Coach and Lorelie. I wanted them to have a prepared meal they didn't have to fuss with. Something simple." She frowned. "I also wanted them to come home to a clean house."

She supposed she could still do her cleaning even if Wade was the only one there. Or even if he left, there would probably be field hands still out back. With a ranch the size of Coach's, there was usually someone around. But it didn't seem right to start without seeing Coach and Lorelie first.

"Why are you cleaning? That's not your job. You already said you're in pain from your other jobs."

She tuned into his hard-edged questions and her frown grew. "No, I said I have a plan for managing my pain. It doesn't rule me unless I let it. Some people have issues much worse than mine. I just have a tricky back. I'm young, able-bodied. Coach needs help. You're helping him. So are the other guys."

"Yes, we are. But this is different. And we're not injured."

She braced a hand on her hip. "How is it different?"

"I don't want you to ever be in the position to have to sweep someone else's floors. It killed me to see you doing it as a kid."

"It was an honest job for honest pay. My mother managed to dig herself out of a pile of debt that way. It was the first business she started, and now she runs a successful restaurant. Not all of us sing for our supper, Bennett."

He set his jaw and opened the screen door with his hip. "Come inside and we'll have this discussion where it's cool. And you can sweep or do whatever you have your mind set on doing while I drink some lemonade. Turns out I've been doing some sweeping and mucking out of stalls this afternoon myself."

Before she could reply, he let the screen door flap shut behind him.

She shook her head and debated heading back to her car. She really didn't need to get into it with him—not about this subject, or about what had almost gone down between them the other night. What she needed was to call her girlfriends and forget all about this failed gesture on her part.

But Coach and Lorelie weren't home and probably wouldn't be for a while yet. If she wanted to tidy up for them, this would be an ideal time to do it. And she could ogle shirtless Wade for a bit longer while he probably ogled her bent over in her short skirt.

That fact really didn't bother her as much as it should have.

Throwing back her shoulders, she strode inside and found Wade shrugging into a denim shirt in the kitchen. The picnic basket sat on the table, surprisingly untouched. Unless he'd shoved a sandwich in his pants, which seemed unlikely. No room to spare in those suckers.

"Decided to cover up?" She wasn't disappointed about that fact. No way.

His smirk indicated he thought otherwise. "I thought I should if we were going to have a serious discussion."

"Who said we were?"

"Me. Or at least I'm hoping we can." He pulled out a chair. "Please sit."

She sat, because he had a way of making her feel about ten inches tall and full of attitude. Sure, she had reasons to be annoyed with him, but maybe her hurt feelings were causing her to blow them out of proportion. She probably wouldn't have been nearly as indignant about his relatively innocent comments on the porch if she'd gotten some the other night.

That was neither here nor there.

He sat across from her, shirt still half unbuttoned, and rested his elbow on the table. It was only then that she saw the deep welts from fatigue under his eyes. "About the other night…"

"Don't. Let's just put it aside, okay?"

"No, not okay. You completely misunderstood my reasoning. Which I get, because I've never been real clear when it comes to you." He pinched the bridge of his nose. "I didn't want to 'hide' us for my sake but for yours. I didn't want you to have to deal with anyone making comments because of the Colt situation. It's not fair to expect you to put up with getting grief from people when I don't live in this town any longer. Whatever they say to me it won't affect me nearly as long as it will you. Your whole life is here."

"And yours is not." Amidst everything he'd said—and she wasn't sure she'd *ever* heard him say so much at one time—that was the most salient point, and one she'd do well to remember. No matter her issues with him, they were temporary. He didn't live in Quinn. Judging from how often he'd come back over the years, he wouldn't be visiting much either.

Even if they had a hot and heavy affair, it would be just that. Maybe he'd write a song about it afterward, for that extra little kick in the butt. She'd get to replay what she'd lost every time she turned on her radio, because the local country station had Wade on constant repeat.

But hell, better to think about what she'd lost than dwelling on *what if*. She'd always wondered what it would be like to be with Wade. Not just the sex part, but actually *being* with him. To have him as her man, for a weekend or a week.

She just couldn't expect anything more.

"No, it isn't." His eyes and tone were heartbreakingly gentle. "I know you've always been a forever kind of girl, Charli, but I guess I'm asking you if you could make a few nights into forever with me."

She sniffled. Must be allergies. Before she knew what was happening, that sniffle turned into a mist in her eyes. She blinked it away and it still kept coming.

Worse, he saw that mist turn into actual tears that dripped down her cheeks, too fast for her hands to catch them.

"Aww, honey, don't do that. I never wanted to make you cry."

"Well, you did. Not just today." She nearly said more, nearly laid it all on the line. Some spiteful part of her ached to blame him for the mess her life had become, though she knew it wasn't fair. She'd made her own choices, as had he. All in all, that messy life had actually turned out pretty great.

But years ago, when she'd been suffering from morning sickness and trying to reconcile having a baby with a man she had great affection for but wasn't in love with—well, it had been damn easy to blame Wade Bennett. He'd gone off for his own happy ending without her. Even if she was pretty sure he would say she'd done that to him first by hooking up with Colt.

God, all she'd wanted was for Wade to make a move. It had been stupid of her to respond to Colt's advances when she already had her sights set elsewhere, but she and Wade had never deviated from the friend zone.

They'd come close a few times. Danced together a bit too tightly at the school dances. Held hands now and then while walking home after a few hours at the library. Sang a couple of duets while Wade strummed his guitar that almost led to kisses.

Almost covered the progression of their relationship well. And at sixteen, she hadn't been patient enough to wait.

She hadn't been patient enough to wait when Colt came back from his stint in the NFL either. He'd been sweet and sexy and oh so attentive. Wade had been long gone by that point, so why not? And one night they'd recklessly made a baby that changed the whole course of their lives, even after it was gone.

Now she was twenty-nine and she still couldn't find enough patience to wait one more day to take Wade up on the offer in his summer-blue eyes.

"A few nights of forever sounds like a dream come true," she said, wondering if she'd grow to regret those words.

Not really giving a damn when Wade scooted his chair around the table so he could cup her cheek in his big hand and draw her closer, almost into his lap.

To hell with *almost*.

Without hesitation, she straddled his thighs and drove her hands into all his thick golden hair. He hadn't cut it in a while and the damp locks spilled through her fists like trapped sunlight. She used them for leverage to tip his mouth exactly where she wanted it and with her eyes wide open, touched her lips to his.

Fire. It was the biggest cliché there was, but God, when his soft lips rubbed over hers before his tongue insistently sought entrance, she couldn't think of anything but the heat scorching her from the inside out. This particular blaze had been set on simmer for so many years, nearly going out. All it took was the skim of his palm over her cheek and the seductive slide of his tongue over hers to have it raging back to life.

His hands coasted down her back, ending up on her ass. He held her in place, right on his rigid cock, and she was helpless to stop from grinding against him. His groan broke in her mouth, a sound of unforgiving need, and she fed it right back to him, moaning under the onslaught of his lips and his hands inching under her sundress to cup her bare bottom. Almost bare, because she'd worn her one and only thong to avoid panty lines.

Then his fingers were prying the thin strip of soaked fabric aside and traveling along the seam of her swollen lower lips. She made a noise of encouragement in her throat, the only one she could manage while his tongue tangled with hers, but he took the hint and pressed one long finger over her clit, holding it still for so long that she gave in to the urge to move faster. She rocked back and forth until the blinding ache inside her gave way to a release so pure and warm that she would've sworn they stood outside under a hot spring. She cried out as he continued to caress her, making her pleasure go on and on.

And after, there was blessed silence, except for the music of their hushed, heavy breathing, mixing and mingling together like life.

Like a wish she'd never dared to make. The sky simply couldn't hold that many stars.

"You're beautiful." He ran the hand not still buried between her legs up her damp cleavage to her throat, pausing to stroke her lower lip with his thumb as his eyes searched hers. Probing so deeply, leaving no part of her unexamined.

With any other man, she'd hate that feeling. With him, it felt natural. Right. He *should* know all of her. Her biggest regret was that he hadn't gotten the chance, and vice versa.

But now they had a new chance. A forever built on a string of nights. And wasting even one of them would be a crime.

"I could say all sorts of things about how you make me feel beautiful," she began shakily, "but the truth is that it'd be impossible not to feel like a rock star after an orgasm like that." She lightly pounded his chest until his serious look gave way to a smile. "Twelve years pent-up. Twelve *years*. Do you understand how horny I am right now?"

His eyes darkened, flashing like the Texas sky before a sudden squall. She expected him to mention Colt, to break the moment. Instead all he did was lift her up and turn her around, settling her on his knees while he fumbled behind her. She tried to turn her head to see what he was doing, but the crinkle of foil delivered the message fast.

Her cheeks blasted with heat and she took a quick glance at the closed back door. Was it locked? God, she hoped so. "We're in Coach's kitchen."

"You just realizing that, darlin'?"

His lazy drawl made her fight back a shiver. "Okay, so I got a little carried away. But this…"

"This isn't going to take more than a few minutes. This time." He eased down his zipper and she gave up trying not to shiver. Lost cause. "Lorelie and Coach will be gone for hours yet," he added, shifting her against him so he could press kisses to the back of her neck.

And oh shit, she'd forgotten how sensitive she was there. His lips kindled sparks that his tongue only coaxed higher as he worked his way around to nibbling on her earlobe. He sucked it into his mouth, making the little triangle earrings she wore clink against his teeth. All the while his hands were on the move, sliding up her dress, easing aside her panties and then…then, oh God, the head of his swollen cock notched against her still overstimulated pussy and she couldn't hold back a moan.

A loud one.

"That sound," he murmured, his warm breath fanning over the damp paths his kisses had left. "So sexy."

"Who else is here?" she asked as he levered up her hips and pushed that much farther inside her. There was going slow and then there was the trip Wade was taking her on, which made molasses traveling uphill seem fast. He

inched deeper, adding the slightest swivel of his hips, and
she bit her lip, about to close her eyes and say fuck it.

Fuck me.

If she couldn't see, could only feel, it didn't really
matter if someone came in and caught them, now did it?
Besides, she couldn't deny there was a certain thrill to
being so wanton and wild right in the middle of the
afternoon in...

Coach's kitchen. Coach, for God's sake.

"Wade," she said urgently. "Who else is—"

"Just think about you and me. Hang on." His big hand
spanned her belly as he pulled her back onto his cock,
finally driving in all the way to the hilt and loosening the
scream she hadn't realized had been building in her throat.
He growled, the sound sending shockwaves of arousal
through her tightening core.

Then he started to move, slow and sure, and if she
hadn't been lost before, she was then. Completely and
totally.

She'd been with men who talked dirty, and men who
didn't. Men who made lots of noises, and men who stayed
utterly silent. She'd only had a handful of lovers, but they'd
run the gamut. Or so she thought until she had sex with
Wade. He did something different.

He kissed her the entire time.

Lips on the back of her neck, on the shoulder bared to
his mouth once he tugged down her dress, on the tops of
her arms. And then when his hips began to drive up into her
harder, faster, the head of his cock scraping that most secret
place inside her, he dragged her back and latched his mouth
onto her jaw, as if he could suck her throbbing pulse right
out of her body. She couldn't moan, couldn't cry out, as his
free hand slipped under her dress and found her clit. His
fingers lazily massaged her while he pounded out a rhythm
inside her that they could both hear.

He began singing to her, as softly as a lullaby, as hypnotic as a movie score. His lips rubbed her skin while he etched the words inside her, branding them so deep she feared she'd never be able to erase them.

On a summer night, I found you there.
All alone with his hands in your hair.
And I believed once that dreams came true.
Until the day I lost you.

His breathing faltered when she reached down to clutch the back of his hand through her dress, holding him to her as she struggled against the pleasure that wanted to drag her under. She shouldn't be more turned on by the song he'd chosen to sing, one she'd heard on the radio dozens of times. She owned a copy too. *Dreamchaser*, Wade's first hit single. She'd wondered all along if it could possibly be about her, about them, before dismissing the idea.

During Colt's NFL years, when she and Colt weren't together, Wade hadn't so much as sent a postcard or called to say hello. He'd known his brother was gone, and he'd still chosen to stay away. Maybe he'd figured it was already too late.

But now he was back, even temporarily, and the poignancy of his song only made her crest that much more rapidly. She held his swiftly circling fingers against the heart of her while she squeezed him deep, silently urging him to take her even harder.

He obliged.

Still singing, the words turning husky as he panted them directly into her ear, he grabbed her hip and powered upward, causing her thighs to shake from the sheer force of his thrusts. Her pussy clamped down on him and he made a strangled noise in his throat, barely skipping a beat. His cock hammered out the bass and his lyrics made her soar higher, because even as terribly painful the song was, now she knew it was for her and that made all the difference.

He'd cared. She'd meant something to him. And now they had another chance.

Once more his shaft brushed that hidden part inside her and this time, she couldn't hold back. A cry tumbled from her, the sound cutting off when he pulled his fingers from between her legs and slipped them between her lips. She sucked on them to muffle her moans as she rode him fast enough to send the chair skidding over the tiles into the table before he stopped it with a boot planted firmly on the floor. She tasted herself on his fingers and licked them clean, grasping his hand in both of hers as he battered her with his cock and his last frantic lyrics battered her soul.

One more day with you is the wish I'd make.
If I had any wishes left to give.
Until then my chances I'll take.
With this life I have left to live.

His erection swelled inside her, stretching her oversensitized walls, and she knew he was close. Releasing his hand, she dug her nails into his thighs and rotated her hips, bearing down until his breath hissed out in a fractured stream against her cheek. Groaning, he pushed into her one last time, holding her still to receive every pulse of his cock into the condom.

She shuddered, her body rallying for one last mini orgasm that trembled around him as he spent himself into the latex. Then he dropped his forehead to her back and curled his arms around her waist, so tightly that she almost couldn't breathe.

She was too happy and grateful to get to share this moment with him to care.

CHAPTER FOUR

"Scoot that a little closer. Now tip it up. A bit more. There you go." Charlene swept a small pile of dust out of the corner of Coach's kitchen—the very kitchen they'd made love in not two hours ago—into the dustpan Wade held at the ready.

If he'd ever had an odder experience post-sex, he didn't remember it. Then again, he didn't remember having better sex, either. That's because he hadn't. Not even close.

Now he was playing wingman to her cleaning general, and laughing more than he thought was possible. The more annoyed she got at what she called his "lackadaisical ways", the more amused it made him.

Damn, she was cute. And sexy as hell when she bent over in that flirty little sundress. At just the right angle, he could see the bottom curve of her sweet behind. He'd had that behind in his hands and pressed against his groin and all it had done was make him hungry for more.

So much more.

"Okay, dump that in the bin and tie off the bag to pile it up with the others." She cocked her head and studied the windows with their pretty gingham curtains. His ma had curtains just like that in her kitchen.

At least she had the last time he'd been home, which was way too long ago. He'd have to go see her and his dad soon. He'd called upon arriving in town, but calling wasn't the same as visiting in person. As she'd told him sternly before lecturing him about making time for his brother and sister too.

Hollie wouldn't be a problem. He loved his kid sister more than life and had already made plans to pick her up after her shift at the library one day next week so they could spend the evening together. Bowling, eating pizza, watching crappy movies. Just chilling like they used to do in the old days.

He imagined he'd be doing some of the same with his old high school buddies too. Tomorrow night he'd swing by Pitchers bar and see what was what. Before then, he'd go by the ranch and see his family. All of his family, including Colt.

But tonight was all about Charlene. Beautiful Charlene who was leaning on her broom and frowning at him with that pucker between her eyebrows that always made him want to kiss it away. This time he could.

"Penny for your thoughts," he teased, letting his lips linger on the spot longer than was necessary. That dang peach scent that clung to her skin was going to be the death of him.

He lifted his arm and sniffed at his sleeve. Now it clung to *his* skin too. Liniment. Who would've thunk it?

"What are you doing? Checking to see if your deodorant failed?"

"Very funny. Actually I wanted to be sure I smelled like you. I have the sudden inexplicable need to eat peaches right off the tree." He pulled her closer and brushed a kiss over the top of her head. "Just let the sticky juice get all over me."

Watching her blush and knowing he'd caused it had to be the best feeling in the world. He'd been nominated for three Grammys, had four gold albums and two platinum, and none of those experiences could touch the simple joy of seeing her so relaxed and unguarded as she snuggled closer. "I have a feeling that's a sexual innuendo. If so, please keep it up."

He laughed. So Charli liked a bit of dirty talk, hmm? It wasn't his specialty—he tended to fall back on lyrics when he had too much to get out of his head and heart—but for her, he'd try.

Forever in a few nights meant pulling out all the stops.

He rubbed the top of her arm, letting his fingers nudge the side of her breast. He hadn't even touched them yet, never mind see them. What a frigging waste, one he would be rectifying soon. "What do you say we take our trash bags and split before Coach and Lorelie get back? We've already left them quite a surprise."

Boy, had they. Charli was one heck of a taskmaster. They'd cleaned the first floor damn well in two hours, no matter what she thought.

She eyed the window behind them and tugged her lower lip between her teeth. "But that could use a nice—"

"Uh-uh. The place looks great, and if we don't get out of here now, they could walk in anytime." Shamelessly, he let his fingers wander toward one taut nipple. He flicked it casually and studied the flare of color that bloomed on her cheeks. "Besides, you have a date tonight. Didn't you say this was your only full day off from all three jobs this week?"

"I did." She cocked her head, her lips curving. "A date, huh? With anyone I know?"

"Oh yeah." He lowered his mouth to hers. "Someone you know real well." He rubbed his lips over hers. "Even in the biblical sense."

Laughter exploded out of her. "Wade Bennett, I haven't heard that term since high school health class when Mrs. Sweeting said that we should only let someone see our biblical side after marriage, and Johnny Berger said he planned not to have one by then."

"Leave it to Johnny. I'm pretty sure he didn't have a biblical side after sixth grade." He drew on the shiny dark ropes of her hair, already imagining it wrapped around his fists as he drove inside her from behind. "The drive-in's showing a horror movie tonight. Something about a small town bloodbath."

She laughed again. "That's your idea of a date?"

Knowing that she loved horror movies just as much as he did—they'd watched enough of them in high school with Hollie wedged between them on the couch to prove it—he smiled and nodded. "Mmm-hmm. I say we bring this picnic basket you packed and tailgate the movie." He nuzzled her temple. "Maybe even park way in back so we can make out a little after dark."

"I made this food for Coach," she said breathlessly. "We can't just take it."

"C'mere, darlin'. Let me show you something." He grabbed her hand and pulled her over to the fridge before opening the door wide. "I think they're doing just fine," he said drily at her gasp.

The shelves were stuffed with food. Fresh produce and vegetables, low-calorie baked goods and about five different casserole dishes lined the shelves. The neighbors had been great to them, bringing over food ever since Coach's heart attack.

They wouldn't miss Charli's picnic basket, that was for sure.

"Okay, so I guess they're good," she said, stepping back and running a hand over her damp brow. She'd been bustling all over the house and only looked the slightest bit worse for wear. "I still feel bad taking it."

"I see your point." He shut the refrigerator and turned to pick up the picnic basket off the table. "I'll take it, and it'll solve the problem. How's that?"

She grinned and placed her hand in his again once he held out his palm. "You're incorrigible."

"Nah, just hungry. Those sandwiches look delicious." He hoisted the picnic basket higher and took a sniff at the top of the basket. "Is that fried chicken I smell?"

"Some nose you have, Strings." Damn, that nickname. Hearing it fall from her pretty lips had him going hard in an instant. She noticed too, her smile turning lewd as she

64

inclined her chin below his waist. "Wow, I never knew you were so fond of chicken."

"Lots of things you didn't know I was fond of," he said lightly, not intending to bring that subject up now. Maybe ever. The mild bondage games he enjoyed in the bedroom weren't necessarily something he intended to broach with Charli. They only had two weeks, and he had no intention of pushing her somewhere she might not want to go.

Spending time with her at all was enough of a gift.

"Is that so?" She tipped back her head, her eyes firing with interest as they headed toward the front door. "I'd like to hear more."

Well then. Most likely she didn't have the first clue what he was indicating, but perhaps he should give her a hint later on—just in case their interests matched up between the sheets as well as their personalities meshed out of them.

So far so good on that score.

"I'd love to tell you more." He kissed her hair and opened the front door before motioning for her to go ahead. "Or show you."

"This date is getting better and better," she said over her shoulder, the laughter in her voice fading as Joel and Oakley, Coach's ranch hands, ascended the front steps. Her face flashed scarlet. "I thought you said no one else was here," she said under her breath.

He waited for her to release his hand and jump back, but she didn't. It impressed him that she was willing to take the heat, even knowing that she'd be taking it alone after he was gone.

Charlene Martinez was one hell of a woman.

"Did I? Don't remember." Turning his smile on the other men, Wade gestured with the picnic basket. "Hey guys. Sorry to bail on you out there. You okay with holding down the fort while Charli and I go catch a flick and a bite to eat? I can come back later if—"

"No, no, we have a houseful already." Joel gestured toward the driveway. "Jackson's back there and he took over where you left off. So no worries about you two kids skipping out." If Joel thought there was anything odd about Wade and Charlene holding hands, he didn't show it. In fact, he looked more interested in the picnic basket. "Hey, is that fried chicken I smell?"

"Cripes, men." With an eyeroll, Charli let go of Wade's hand and turned to dig through the picnic basket that Wade still held. She emerged with a wrapped plate of chicken and thrust it at Joel, ignoring Wade's protest. "Here you go. Share with the guys. You know, all of the guys who were right outside the house." Charli enunciated each word slowly and carefully, causing Wade to grin like a besotted idiot.

He'd made love to his dream girl. Maybe not as slowly or thoroughly as he wished, but he'd have time to rectify that. He would make sure of it.

"Oh yeah. This smells delicious. Thanks, Charlene." Grinning, Joel slapped Oakley on the back and the two guys headed back in the same direction they'd come from, apparently forgetting whatever it was that had caused them to come up to the house.

Amazing fried chicken could wipe a man's thoughts. So could a gorgeous woman propping her hands on her hips and narrowing her eyes.

"You lied to me," she said.

"I prefer fibbed, as I didn't exactly say there wasn't anyone outside. I just wanted you to focus on us. Like I was doing." He stepped closer to caress her cheek. "A bomb could've gone off and I never wouldn't heard or seen anyone but you."

"You, Wade Bennett, are a sweet talker." Her anger was already melting, just as she was softening under his

Going Long

touch. He loved seeing the effect he had on her, knowing she affected him the same damn way. "Serves you right that you have one plate less of chicken."

"One plate less?" He took a hopeful glance at the picnic basket. "There's more?"

Her lips twitched. "Yes. And you can have some later, after I go home and shower and get presentable for our date."

He bumped his hip against hers. "I need to get presentable too. Don't suppose you'd mind sharing your shower with a humble public servant?"

She snorted and shook her head. "That's a new one, I gotta hand you that. But yes, you can share my water." Turning, she tossed him a saucy glance over her shoulder before heading down the steps. "Just don't think you can take too many liberties. I'm a prim and proper girl."

"Since when?" Unable to resist, he leaned forward to swat her ass. Gripping her behind, she let out a yelp that quickly turned into a blush that made him hard all over again.

Unless he was very mistaken, Charli hadn't minded being spanked. And that was something he intended to investigate very soon.

Two hours later, freshly showered, freshly sexed and fully satiated—when it came to food, at least—Wade pulled up to the Midway Drive-In and let out a low whistle at the long line of cars waiting to take a spot on the wide field in front of the projection screen. "Guess I won't have to search for a spot in the back. Looks like that's about the only option available to us."

"It's date night. You know people in Quinn like their movies."

"I do, but I never guessed *Blood Spatter* would be such a hit with the hometown crowd." Tossing her a grin, he eased off on the gas and flipped the radio to another station. He didn't have fancy satellite radio or a Bluetooth hookup

67

to his iPod or any of that. His local stations suited him just fine.

Except when they were playing his music.

"Aww, will you look at that? Mr. Wade Bennett crooning on the radio." Flashing him a flirtatious grin, she turned up the volume and started to sing along with the recorded track in her husky, seductive voice. "That's one of my favorites," she said with a sigh when the song ended.

He gaped at her. "You know my songs?"

"Like the menu at Rosa's. Backwards, forwards and sideways." Her grin faded under the intensity of his stare. "Yes. I buy the CDs as soon as they come out. I load them up on my iPod. I leave it on the country channel 24/7 in case they happen to play you—which they do, a lot. Any more questions, cowboy?"

Wade tightened his grip on the wheel. "What did Colt think about that?"

"He didn't have a problem with it, since he's proud of you too. All of us are here. You might've been in a hurry to outrun Quinn, but Quinn never wanted to let go of you."

"No one ever shamed me as well as someone with the last name Martinez," he said quietly. "Usually it was Rafe knocking some sense into me. Once, it was your mama. First time it's ever been you."

She shifted in her seat and tugged down the short dress she'd thrown on after their mutual shower. She hadn't taken more than five minutes with her clothes and makeup, but he'd never seen a lovelier woman. "When did my mama do it?"

Not wanting to go there right now, he stretched his arm along the back of her seat and maneuvered the truck forward as the line of cars crept along. "Charli—"

"Don't 'Charli' me. When?"

The memory of that day came back to him as clear as the sun beaming through his windshield. "A few weeks before I left."

He'd switched out of the regular high school program into G.E.D. classes right after their championship football season had ended, intending to shave off a couple of months so he could get to Nashville that much quicker. Instead of feeling nostalgic about the upcoming end of his high school career, he'd been in a rush to put a period on it that much faster.

Putting a period to watching Colt and Charlene walk around hand-in-hand had been another bonus.

"What did she say?" she asked, stiffening under the hand he dropped to her shoulder.

He shut his eyes for a moment, the sun suddenly way too bright. "That you needed someone to count on, and if I was the good friend I claimed to be, I'd make your choice easier." Charli made a sound in her throat and he let out a hollow laugh. "Fuck, I didn't even realize there *was* a choice. No one had ever picked me over my brother. Once he came onto the field, I fell into the support role. That's the way it had always been, and I was okay with it." *Except when it came to you.* "But just in case somehow my presence was conflicting you, I knew I needed to get gone as fast as possible. It's what I wanted anyway," he added.

"She never should have said that." Charli balled her hands into fists. "She had no right."

"Your mama was just looking out for you, like she always did. That's what mothers do."

"*Your* mother has hated me since I was seventeen because you kissed me goodbye. I didn't even know it was coming yet it was all my fault."

He diverted his attention from the line of cars inching forward to study her face. "What are you talking about?"

"You kissed me goodbye at that stupid going-away party of yours, remember? We were out back, near the barn." At his nod, she hissed out a breath. "Your mom saw us through the window. She saw me put my hands in your hair. Hell, she probably even saw me grope your ass."

"I don't remember that part." She hit him lightly on the arm but he didn't laugh. He couldn't. "I do remember. I remember every second of that kiss."

"I'm glad, because I never stopped paying for it. Even after Colt came back from the NFL and we got together—hell, even after I got pregnant—"

Wade inhaled, sucking all the air out of the cabin so fast he was amazed he managed not to gasp. "You got pregnant? When?"

Her eyes widened. "You didn't know?"

"No. I didn't. No one ever told me." He scratched his scruffy jaw and waited until he was reasonably certain his voice would be level. "What happened to the baby?"

Colt's baby. She'd had a baby with his brother.

"I miscarried at nine weeks. Barely enough time for—"

"Plenty of time for a lot," he interjected, hating that soft, halting quality to her voice. He would bet he wasn't the only one who couldn't take in enough air.

To try to help them both, he cranked the A/C up one more notch. And waited.

"We got married because of the baby. I told Colt as soon as I knew."

"I'm so sorry, darlin'. For both of you." He wondered why Colt had never mentioned it to him, then decided he probably already knew. Wade hadn't been much of a brother to him over the years. It hadn't been intentional, and Wade had tried to show up when he could. Damn, it had been tough to be part of family events with Colt and Charli. He'd waited for the passing of time to ease the sting, and it had some, but not nearly enough.

By the time he'd begun to grow accustomed to the idea of their marriage, they'd separated. And that stupid, stubborn, utterly foolish hope had sprouted in Wade's heart once again.

Now he'd have to mend fences, and hope it wasn't too late. That was if he hadn't broken them irreparably with the action he'd taken that very afternoon. He wouldn't blame his brother if Colt never wanted to speak to him again once he found out what had happened.

Some lines just shouldn't ever be crossed.

"In retrospect, maybe I should've held off telling him until the end of the first trimester," she said quietly. "Or maybe I should've said no when he proposed. I knew it was mostly because he wanted to do the right thing for the baby. We both wanted that."

As much as a part of him—a small, uncharitable part—wanted to rejoice that her marriage hadn't been the nirvana he'd assumed, he knew that was wrong. He cared about her so much. He always had, even after she'd married Colt. God knows he loved his brother, even if he hadn't been the best at showing that over the years. He'd never wanted them to be miserable.

No, he'd come to terms with that as *his* lot in life, and had accepted early on that he might as well learn to play violin with all the whining he was doing in his own head.

"You did what you were meant to do. Regrets are useless and cheapen what the two of you had together. I know you had some happy times with Colt, because I saw them."

"You mean during those hour-long visits you managed every year or so? Hard to get a real good gauge on a marriage that way." When he didn't respond, she grabbed her cold soda, popping the top. "I care a great deal about your brother. He was good to me, and I'd like to hope I was good to him. But I never loved him *that* way. And I'm not sure he ever loved me either. Not the way a husband is supposed to love his wife. So, yeah, regrets. I've got a few." She toasted him with her soda. "Write a song about that, huh? *To All of Charli's Mistakes* would be a fine title."

"I've written other songs for you," he said as the line finally started to move and their vehicle with it.

"The one you sang during...yes."

"During yes?" He shot her a grin, relieved the heavy tension was momentarily broken. "You can say the word sex, honey. It's not a dirty one."

"It is if you do it right." She rolled her sweating soda can over the cleavage exposed by her dress and damn if he didn't almost swallow his tongue. "Which songs have you written about me?"

He saw her lips move, but he wasn't capable of comprehending at that present time.

Finally realizing that, she laughed and slid the can down a tad farther, rolling down the top of her dress with it. He glimpsed pale pink satin beneath and had to shift on his seat. Christ.

"Keep going," he murmured. "We won't be at the front of the line for a few minutes yet."

"Wade..." She trailed off, biting her generous lower lip. Making his cock harder than ever.

"You know you want to tease me. Just like you used to do in those short-as-hell cheerleading skirts back in school."

"I didn't know you ever noticed me in mine."

"Oh, I noticed. I wasn't the only one. Half the guys on the team were a little in love with you. But no one dared go where Colt had planted his flag."

Her teasing expression vanished, and he wanted to cut off the tongue he'd nearly swallowed. That was it. No more mentions of Colt tonight. He had nothing to do with him and Charli right now. This was all about them.

"I'll have you know that Colt didn't 'plant his flag' until after he came back from the NFL. I was a virgin all that time." She made a face. "My mama told me to save myself for my husband, and then I slept with Colt, thinking

I was finally turning reckless. Kick in the ass there, huh? Sleeping with him *got* me a husband."

He laughed and reached across the center console to take her free hand. "It's kind of amazing, don't you think?"

"What?" she asked warily.

"That even after all these years, we can sit here together and still be friends. *More* than friends," he said, rubbing his thumb over her knuckles.

"You were the best friend I ever had."

He smiled. "Same. Don't tell your brother I said that, though."

"I won't unless I need to for bribery purposes. Which songs, Wade?"

It was hard not to shift around like a schoolboy presenting the girl he was sweet on with a valentine, but he tried to keep his face stoic. "*One Night In Texas* and *Riverbend.*"

"No way. *Riverbend* is my favorite." She bent down to dig through his old school CD case. "We have to listen to it now."

"I don't have it here."

"What? Okay, so we'll listen to *One Night In Texas* then. Or even your first CD—" She broke off as she flipped through the clear plastic pages in the case he'd had since the beginning of time. Probably since high school. "You don't have any of them. Not one."

He cleared his throat. "Nah. Who wants to listen to their own music? Boring."

But he had, once. When the music had still been his. Now it felt like he was being sucked up into some giant corporate machine that only wanted a facsimile of Wade Bennett, not the real deal.

"It's great stuff. How can you call it boring?"

If he told her how he really felt—that listening to his old music made him alternately wistful and angry—she'd just ask more questions. And by God, they only had a week and a half left before he had to go back to Nashville to face the mess he'd left behind. He needed an escape. He needed *her* as she should always be—happy, free and playful. Not worried with that little wrinkle between her eyes, no matter how cute it was.

"I'll sing *Riverbend* to you after the movie." He reached over to cup her knee. "When we're all alone."

She didn't seem all that placated. "You better keep that promise."

"I will. You can count on it," he said, rolling down his window as they finally reached the ticket stand.

Two hours later, the horror movie was winding down, and the sun was on the verge of setting. Beautiful yellows, oranges and pinks streaked the sky above the projection screen where the sole survivor of the bloodbath had tearfully thrown herself into the cop's arms. The cop would probably be her love interest in *Blood Spatter Two*. Even horror liked its love stories.

He cuddled Charlene against his chest as she shivered, adjusting the blanket he'd been sure they wouldn't need over her legs. An old quilt cushioned the truck beneath them. The wind had kicked up, turning surprisingly cool as sunset approached.

They'd enjoyed the fine meal she'd packed in her picnic basket during the movie. While they didn't have the best seat in the house vantage-wise, he couldn't argue with the privacy angle. They were situated near a leafy copse of trees, so far back that only a few vehicles were nearby. The sides of the truck bed had offered just enough cover for him to feel comfortable slipping a hand under Charlene's skirt and giving her an orgasm between murders two and three.

And when Charli had screamed, so had lots of others. She'd just had a different reason.

Now he was ready to give her another orgasm, better than the last. This time she'd be riding his cock.

As the credits rolled, she sat up and stretched. "Wow. Gory."

"Didn't like it?"

She grinned. "No. It was awesome."

"That's my girl. Glad to see you still love horror movies after all this time. What else do you still love?"

She snuggled against his chest again, obviously getting the hint that he didn't plan on moving anytime soon. Let the other vehicles clear out fast. Parked in front of a setting sun, with a warm Texas breeze cooling their skin and his dream girl in his arms, seemed like a mighty fine place to be.

"Hmm, well, I still love Mexican food. My mama's chimichangas and deep fried ice cream especially. I still love doing high kicks and cartwheels and all that stuff when my back allows it."

He toyed with the long strands of her hair. She'd freed it from its ponytail and the curls whipped across her face in the growing wind, catching on her glossy lips. He shifted his hips away from her, not wanting her to know how swiftly his thoughts had detoured south again.

She'd find out soon enough.

"You still have your cheerleading uniform?"

"Yes, I still have it, and I still fit into it too. Usually. Depends how much deep fried ice cream I've indulged in that month." She smiled. "I still love hanging out with your sister at the library. It still has the best A/C in all of Quinn. Swimming in the lake with the girls. Handy that Lela lives right on the lake. Even more handy now that you're staying there too." Her smile deepened until she showed off her dimples. A rare and treasured sighting. "I still love dancing my ass off in the rain—"

"Since when? And how come I didn't know this about you?"

"A girl has to have some secrets," she said, canting her head to the side and batting her eyelashes.

"Uh-huh. Keep going."

"I still love listening to you sing," she murmured, inching closer until the words blew over his mouth. "Especially love when you're moving inside me while you're singing in my ear. Hottest thing ever."

"Oh no, darlin'. Sorry to say that's not even close." He cupped her cheek and drew her face up to his so they were eye-to-eye in the waning light. "You ever done it in a truck?"

"No. Have you?"

"Unfortunately not. People 'round here give me space. They're understanding. But sometimes I get recognized when I travel other places. Gotta be really careful what I do where." He brushed her hair back and gathered it into a loose ponytail at the nape of her neck. "And with who. It has to be someone I trust."

"You trust me, Strings?" She dipped her head and nipped his jaw. "What if I want to take a couple of pictures to remember you by?"

His heartbeat quickened from the combination of her biting kisses and her questions. She was a dirty girl down deep, and damn if that didn't turn him on more.

"What kind of pictures are you talking about?"

"Naked ones. Just you and your guitar." She licked his throat. "Maybe one with your hat hiding the private parts so I could use it as the background on my phone."

"You want me on your phone, huh?"

"I want you everywhere."

He pulled her closer and hoisted her leg up higher on top of both of his. Then he let his hand wander under the hem of her dress to the edge of her panties. "That so?"

"Mmm-hmm."

"You want me inside you out here, where anyone can see?"

She didn't even hesitate. "God yes."

"Fingers first," he said, slipping two underneath the cotton. "I warmed you up before, now I want to see how hot you can run."

"Hot enough you better watch how close you get to the fire."

He sank his fingers inside her, bypassing her clit entirely. She gasped and shifted, lifting her leg slightly to give him more access. The field was quickly clearing out, a long line of vehicles headed out of the area. Someone shouted about the threat of rain, which pleased him immensely. He lowered his head to speak into her ear. "You said you like to dance in the rain. How do you feel about dancing on my cock?"

"Dancing, huh? That's a new one." She let out a throaty chuckle that turned into a moan when he pressed deeper and curved his fingers upward. "Ahh, God, don't stop."

"Never." He rubbed his lips over the top of her ear and swiveled his fingers, being careful that her dress still mostly covered his hand. The moviegoers were taking off, and the threat of discovery was exciting, but he hadn't been joking when he'd mentioned too many people wanting a piece of him. More importantly, they'd get a piece of Charli too, and that couldn't happen.

He had no intention of hiding their relationship while he was in town, but he also didn't want to cause her any more embarrassment than necessary. It was his job to shield her from as much of that as he could. She'd trusted him, and now he would earn it.

But that didn't mean he couldn't push the limits a little.

"Flattery will get you everywhere."

"Not yet, but I'm on my way." He slid his lips along her cheek. "Can you come for me yet, darlin'?"

"Almost." She frowned and intensity flared bright in her eyes for a fraction of a second. "No, dammit, I can."

She curled her leg tighter around both of his and arched upward, giving him the perfect angle to arrow his tongue along the tiny droplets of perspiration on her cleavage. "Sing to me again," she gasped, making his mouth curve against her flesh.

With the constriction in his jeans and the way she was grinding against him, he had to struggle for the right words. Then he didn't have to think anymore and followed his heart, just as Coach had said to do.

I fell for a girl back when love was new.
And had no idea she felt it too.
They say second chances don't wait.
But they did this time, because we're no longer jailbait.

She laughed then muffled the moan that followed against his shoulder. All the while, his fingers kept the beat inside her, steady and sure.

"God, yes. I'm there." Hips pumping, she reared back with the most gorgeous smile on her face, as if the swirling sky above had parted to reveal the setting sun. Her release slickened his hand, so deliciously dirty, and he couldn't get his fly down fast enough.

He wanted to feel her on his skin. All over him.

"That's some song," she said once her breath began to regulate.

"Off the new album. In stores never." He tugged her more fully on top of him and slanted his mouth over hers, hungry to taste the excitement in her kiss. If anything, her hands had grown even more impatient as they tugged open the bottom few buttons on his shirt and streaked underneath to caress his torso. "Ah, fuck, yes. Touch me."

"I want you." She bit his Adam's apple and he jerked, his hard cock—still trapped in his boxers—wedging against the warm cleft of her pussy. Jesus, he needed to get inside her. He'd never grow tired of the feeling of her closing around him. Experiencing it once had just intensified his appetite for more. "Your fingers aren't enough."

"No. Not for me either." Gently fisting a handful of her hair, he turned her head and pressed his cheek to hers. "There are still too many people here. That line of cars…they can probably hear you scream."

"I don't care." She wiggled against him. "Fuck me again, damn you, Wade Bennett. Haven't you made me wait long enough? It's been a long ass time since I've been jailbait."

His laughter burst out of him and she caught it in her mouth, swallowing it down and turning it into something much wilder. Their tongues slashed against each other and he fought to get his boxers down with one hand and to drag her closer with the other. His breathing grew choppy as she took over the task, freeing him from his cotton prison and caging him in with her strong, flexible fingers. One stroke and he was on the verge of begging. Two and he didn't know if he was strong enough to resist pushing her head down to his groin.

God, the hot, wet suction of her throat pulling on his dick would kill him.

"Ride it," he gritted out.

The look she flashed him was pure challenge. "Right here?" she asked, letting the drawl come into her voice. "In front of all these people? Why, Wade Bennett, you're a naughty boy."

"Wallet's in my pocket." He gripped her chin between two fingers and gave her a hard, unforgiving kiss. "You know what to do."

She wasted no time in removing his wallet and taking out a condom. She tore it with her teeth and slicked it down his length with an efficiency that might've impressed him if just the sensation of her fingers brushing his skin hadn't made his balls draw up tight and full.

Glancing around, she wiggled her panties off under her skirt and, after searching for a place to stow them, pushed the tiny scrap of lacy fabric in his shirt pocket like a damn handkerchief. He was still grinning when she flipped up her skirt and shimmied onto his lap, acting perfectly casual. They were just an affectionate pair, out on a date. Cuddling. But instead of allowing her to slide down on his cock as she started to do, he slipped his arm under her legs and set her sideways on his lap.

"We're just snuggling, see?" He adjusted her position, drawing her closer and lining up his straining dick with her slick slit. She gasped and widened her legs just enough to give him access to the snug clasp between her thighs, her whole body jerking as he took aim and hit his target in one long, hard pass. "Oh Christ," he groaned, biting her shoulder to keep from shouting. "You're like a damn virgin. I can't fucking move."

"I can." Eyes glittering, she subtly rotated her hips, her breasts rising and falling in the modest top of her dress. He drew his legs together, bobbling her on her lap, and she cried out, her pussy flexing involuntarily around him. "You're so deep," she whispered as he laid his hand on her lower belly, wanting her to feel every movement he made throughout her body.

"And I'm about to go deeper." He lifted her off his lap and slammed her back down, crushing his mouth to hers as they gasped through her sudden, unexpected orgasm. At least *he* hadn't been expecting it. But as her warm juices flooded his cock, he had no choice but to retreat and enter her again, both to heighten her pleasure and to seek his own.

This would be no marathon fuck. He'd be lucky to get two more strokes off before—

A crack of thunder crashed through the sky and someone let out a distant squeal of surprise. Within seconds, the churning sky opened up and rain gushed down, soaking them to the skin in a minute flat.

Not that either of them cared.

Charli bowed her back, pushing her firm breasts upward. Her nipples were tight little beads he couldn't resist getting in his mouth. The downpour molded her dress to her skin and with every suck, he tasted the rain and inhaled her fresh peachy scent. Sweet. Innocent.

And then she gripped his cock in her silken walls, fisting him so brutally that his vision flashed with the lightning inside his head rather than the bolts slashing across the sky.

"Come on," she whispered, encouraging him, planting her heels on the truck bed to get more leverage while she worked his length. Her voice was a siren's call that rose even above the rain drumming on the top, sides and bed of the truck. That metallic noise offered a beat for him to match as his hips pistoned wildly and he fought to get as deep as he could go, *deeper*, needing to feel her heat clench around him one more time before his control snapped.

"Now," he said, scraping his teeth over her nipple through damp cotton. Her thighs spasmed and she moaned again, clearly chasing another orgasm even as she helped him chase his. Thunder erupted both inside and outside his head, filling the world with jagged colors and sounds. He thrust over and over, riding out his climax with the same single-minded intensity he played his guitar. Wringing the joy from each and every note until the strings fell silent.

Then she turned her head and pressed her mouth to his. "Best raindance ever," she breathed.

CHAPTER FIVE

What a week. She'd certainly ticked her sexual exploit list up a few notches. And the week wasn't over yet.

Among other places, she'd had sex in Coach's kitchen—kind of embarrassing and slightly disrespectful but still hot—and in the bed of a famous singer's truck. Not just any famous singer. Wade Larue Bennett, the object of her teenage fantasies and adult anger. He was both her poison and her cure, her question and her answer.

The man also fucked like a damn stallion.

Smiling to herself, Charlene pulled the car to the curb outside of Rosa's. It was Thursday already, a full week since Wade had come back to town, and boy, had they been making good use of their time together. What little of it there was anyway. They hadn't been able to see nearly enough of each other, due to her long shifts at the store and the restaurant and his long hours helping out at Coach's, but they were making do. And how.

She spent every night in Wade's arms. Kissing, touching, exploring each other with the patience that a dozen years apart had brought. Trading that patience for passion and laughter until night bled into day and the stars winked out, one by one. Sleeping tangled together until her alarm woke them and they stumbled blearily into the shower, already looking forward to meeting at lunch.

Not just meeting. Making love like wild things wherever they could steal a few moments alone.

Yesterday's lunchtime quickie at Wade's lake house rental had been cut short by the stomping around upstairs of two members of Wade's backup band. They were in town for Wade's meeting with some songwriter from Los Angeles, though she could tell Wade just liked having his friends with him. She'd been tempted to ask him if she could meet the band, then decided that maybe it was better if they kept the strings of their personal lives separate. Easier to untie the knots once he'd gone back to reality.

Or so she kept telling herself.

She headed into the restaurant even though it was her day off, determined to speak to her mother. With the whirlwind of the last week, she hadn't had a chance, but she didn't want to wait one more day. What her mother had said to Wade all those years ago needed to be addressed. It had affected three lives in huge ways, and she needed to say her peace. She also needed to state for the record that in case there was any lingering doubt, she was a grown, intelligent woman capable of making up her own mind and making her own choices.

Busy workday or not, it was time she and her mama had it out.

"She's not here," Juanita, one of the waitresses, said as soon as Charlene entered the restaurant. "She went to deliver lunch to your brother at his office. You know how Rafe gets when he's in the middle of 'something big'." Juanita's air quotes made Charlene smile in spite of herself.

"How long ago did she leave?"

"You just missed her."

Charlene sighed. Her luck appeared to be holding. No luck at all, that is. "Okay, thanks. Can you ask her to call me? And if that pigheaded oaf brother of mine shows his face here, tell him to call me too. I've been trying to reach him for weeks."

More so the past week, because she'd been hoping she and Rafe and Wade could spend some time together, just like the old days. Naturally Rafe had been hunkered down in his office and incommunicado. True, it might be a little weird now for Rafe since she and Wade were hooked up. Her older brother had always been insanely protective of her, but for God's sake, she was an adult. She didn't need to be handled or managed or coddled.

She could have an adult affair with a man she cared about and walk away when it was over with her heart intact. It wasn't even a thing.

She wouldn't let it be.

"Sure thing. Do you want some chicken tortilla soup? Made fresh." Juanita pinched Charlene's hip. "You're getting too skinny."

Charlene laughed right out loud. "My scale says otherwise, but yes, thank you. I'll take it to go."

"Be right back."

While she waited, she pulled out her cell and noted she had a voicemail from her brother—*sorry, been busy, we'll talk soon, I promise*—and a text from Wade. Actually no. It was a picture. Eyebrows knitted, she waited for her crappy signal to load the image.

And then nearly dropped her phone.

He'd sent her a dick shot. Okay, not exactly. More like a hint of dick. Basically it was just a snap of his drum-tight abs and his unbuttoned jeans and the happy trail that led to a definite bulge. She could only see the tip of him peeking out over the top of his boxers but it was enough. Her mouth watered and she blushed sixteen shades of red, she was sure.

"Here you go, bebe."

Charlene jumped and tucked the phone back in her purse. Dear Lord, she hoped Juanita hadn't noticed the picture. Not that the penis was identifiable, but still. That man.

That hot as hell, freaking *insane* man.

"Thank you. Mmm, it smells—"

"Dios mio, you're blushing. No, no, not just blushing." The other woman pushed Charlene's hair out of her face. "Flushed right up to the hairline. What has gotten into you?"

"Nothing. I'm just happy."

She was, she realized. Stupidly so. She knew it wouldn't last long—that it couldn't, because a fling by definition meant short and temporary—but she couldn't help smiling. It had been so long since she'd felt this way about a man. The low buzz of attraction under her skin, the distracted thoughts and the eagerness to see him again all added up to one irrefutable fact.

She had it bad.

"I can see that." Juanita took her arm and tugged her into a slightly more private corner a short distance from the entrance. "Who is he?"

"What?"

"You know what. A man's put that glow in your cheeks, and I want to know who."

Charlene shook her head. "No one. Really. I'm just in a good spot right now."

"I know you've always been a forever kind of girl, Charli, but I guess I'm asking you if you could make a few nights into forever with me."

She would never forget Wade's words as long as she lived. And maybe part of making forever out of a few days meant taking the chance of walking in the sunshine with the man she cared so much about.

They were more to each other than amazing quickies at lunch and rough rides in trucks. They were best friends who fed each other Chinese on chopsticks and laughed over Bullwinkle cartoons and curled together in bed at night because spending every minute they had together now that they'd found each other again didn't seem like enough. The clock was ticking, and she wanted whatever bits of her forever she could grab.

"I'm seeing someone," she said carefully, swallowing over the dryness in her throat.

"Ooh, I knew I recognized that sparkle in your eye. Your mama will be so happy. Anyone I know?"

"Yes. Wade Bennett."

Juanita's smile faded. "The big singer? Colton's..."
She trailed off. "Oh my."

"Yes. Oh my. Wade is my ex-husband's brother, and
yes, I know what I'm doing." She didn't, not really, but
she'd harbored a brief, foolish hope that maybe Juanita
wouldn't look at her as if she'd beheaded a chicken in the
middle of the restaurant. That maybe her old friend would
keep smiling and fussing over her, thrilled at the happiness
she'd found.

Even if it was temporary.

God, if she couldn't come clean with Juanita, who had
no stake in the matter, how could she tell all of their old
friends? They were Colt's friends too. Lela was already
starting to speculate. AJ and Randi and Lorelie would be
next. As wonderful as they were, and as open-minded, it
was still an awkward situation, and she didn't want to put
her friends in the middle if Colt reacted badly. The only
one she could be certain would understand was Paige.

At Juanita's silence, Charlene turned away and blinked
away the dampness in her eyes. She should've known this
wasn't the kind of secret she could share.

She hurried to the door and pushed it open, stepping
out into the bright sunshine. At that moment, the adopted
hometown she'd come to love so dearly felt suffocating,
and the picture that had made her so hot and bothered on
her phone felt like contraband she should erase.

"Charlene, wait."

"I'll talk to you later," she said over her shoulder to
Juanita, rushing up the street to her car before the other
woman could flag her down.

Once behind the wheel, she started the engine and
sucked in a couple of deep breaths of cool air. Thank God
for air conditioning on days like this. If she blasted it long
enough, maybe the heat suffusing her cheeks would begin
to fade.

She wasn't ashamed. Not exactly. She was a single woman. She and Colt were long finished, and he'd been with many women since their divorce. But she knew it probably didn't matter that she hadn't slept with anyone in what felt like forever, because of whom she'd chosen to break her streak with.

One glance in the rearview mirror at her own stricken dark eyes had her putting the car in gear. No. She wasn't doing this. She'd finally found a shot at happiness, however brief, and she wasn't going to let anyone steal her thunder. She also wasn't going to make herself feel guilty by continuing to sneak around with Wade. He'd said he wanted to walk in the sunshine with her, but had ultimately left that ball in her court.

Now she was kicking it into center field.

She drove straight to the Bennett ranch and parked near the house. She didn't see Colt's 4x4 but that didn't mean he wasn't inside. Sometimes he walked over from the ranch where he worked with Drake to have lunch with his mom, especially since she'd broken her wrist a few weeks ago. He usually brought her a sandwich or some flowers to brighten her day or just came by to say hello. In spite of him living in one of the outbuildings on the property, which might make him more insistent on protecting his personal space, he never hesitated to make himself available if his mom needed him.

Swallowing hard, Charlene hesitated before climbing out. Colt really was a great guy. Someday he was going to make some woman fabulously happy. She'd wished she was that woman for a long time. But she couldn't help it that she wasn't.

If her beau wasn't Wade, this wouldn't be so uncomfortable. Colt had met one of the few guys she'd dated since the divorce and he'd seemed cool with it. But Wade was…Wade. Even so, she couldn't sit there and wonder while it festered inside her for one more minute.

Hiding the truth wasn't fair to any of them, and she wouldn't do it any longer. Perhaps her coming clean might even encourage Wade to find his way back to talking to Colt again.

She had to try.

Halfway up to the porch, she stopped as the front door flew open and a man in a black cowboy hat stepped out. Not just any man. The man who had taken up residence in her thoughts during all the hours he wasn't in her body over the past week. She even dreamed about him, for God's sake. Now he was smiling down at her from underneath the overhang, saying nothing, just waiting for her to keep walking up to him.

She should be disappointed he was here right now, because that meant she couldn't talk to Colt privately and she figured she owed him that. But she couldn't bring herself to feel anything but joy.

"Fancy seeing you here," Wade drawled, his smile spreading. "You looking for lunch?"

"I already got my appetizer." Lifting a brow, she waved her phone. "Interesting...take on the situation," she added, ascending the porch steps to him.

"I thought so. You said you were busy this afternoon, so I thought I'd give you something to whet your appetite."

"It worked." She stopped directly in front of him—not too close—and glanced at the wide windows before taking a chance and hooking her fingers in his belt loops. "Uh, is Colt here?" At the flash in Wade's eyes, she hastily added, "We need to tell him. *I* need to tell him," she amended. "I know he's your brother, but I feel a responsibility to—"

"You do notice where I'm standing, right?" He gestured around him. "I came here to talk to my folks and Colt if he was around. But apparently he's on a buying trip for his horse training business." He frowned. "How come I didn't know he had a horse training business?"

"Well, you've been mostly out of touch for a while," she said, stroking the inside of his wrist. She just couldn't stop touching him. She also couldn't stop taking surreptitious glances at the door and windows, especially now that she knew that his parents had been appraised.

Assuming they were home.

"How long will Colt be gone for? I really wanted to talk to him."

"Only a couple of days. My ma said he didn't want to go now but there was some sort of issue with a filly he's purchasing in San Antonio." Wade pushed back his hat to pass a hand through his hair. "Christ, I shouldn't have put it off, huh?"

"I understand why you did." She bit her lower lip and stared down at the floor. "I did too."

"Hey. Look at me." He tipped her chin up with a single finger and warmed her with his tender gaze. "We're both feeling our way through this."

"Did you manage to tell your mom at least? Does she hate me?" *Hate me more*, Charlene finished silently.

With a wistful smile, he shook his head. "She's not here. She was on her way out when me and the guys pulled up. Dad was driving her to a doctor's appointment for her wrist and then they had a lunch date with some friends. They offered to cancel but I said I'd catch them later."

"What guys?"

"Glen and Jared. They're back in one of the barns, raising hell." He grinned. "Glen said the acoustics were perfect so he and Jared started messing around on their instruments. Jared even brought his damn banjo. Glen's van is parked around back."

She tried to drum up a smile. They were striking out all over today, weren't they? "Oh. Guess we're not meant to come clean."

"Coming clean makes it sound like we're guilty of something. We aren't. We're both single. We're both adults." He cupped her cheek. "We certainly waited long enough."

"Not everyone will see it that way."

Her girlfriends would have her back. She knew that, deep down. They were incredible people. She just didn't want to put anyone in an untenable position considering Colt.

It shouldn't matter. By the time word had spread— assuming it hadn't already begun making the rounds after the show they'd put on at the movies the other night—she and Wade would be finished.

"Truth is, we don't have to tell anyone we don't want to. I'm not saying we hide," he said when she stiffened. "But there's a difference between hiding and taking out an advertisement in the *Sentinel*, you know?"

"I do know. I also know that I'd like to make this easy on those we care about. As easy as possible."

"I'm gonna be gone in a week, baby." The fact that he delivered those words with more than a little regret didn't alleviate the sharp sting in her throat.

"Do you think I've forgotten that?" She turned away from him to brace her hands on the railing.

"No. Neither of us have." He gripped her waist and brushed his mouth over her shoulder, sending heat curling through her body. "God knows I'd like to."

She didn't say anything. His final remark didn't make the reality any less difficult for her to swallow.

Temporary lovers didn't need to make any big gestures to tell their families and friends. Maybe it was blind luck that had everyone unavailable today. Perhaps the universe wanted them to sweep it all under the rug.

Once Wade had returned to Nashville, it wasn't as if they'd keep this going. How could they, with the distance between them and their time-consuming jobs? He was on the road with God knows how many women throwing themselves at his feet night after night and she barely had time to breathe most of the time. The only reason she'd had enough time to take a long lunch was because she'd gone into the feed store extra early to get caught up on paperwork. Paige handled a lot of it, and had been doing a bit more since Wade had been in town, but the fact was that the store was half Charlene's. She couldn't shirk her work there and she couldn't leave her mama in the lurch at the restaurant. True, business was good and her mother had hired on more help, but it wasn't enough.

Nothing would ever be enough to bridge the miles between her and Wade. They'd had a chance for some fun, and she'd taken it. In a week, she would let go because she had a life to live, and she couldn't go back to waiting for someday. She'd waited for *someday* for the duration of her marriage—*someday it'll be better, someday I won't wonder if I made a mistake, someday we'll be more than just friends who have sex*—and that someday had turned into Colt filing for divorce. Apologetically, of course. It wasn't her, it was him. But he'd done it all the same.

And he'd been right.

"At least I got a hold of Hollie. She's on her way over."

Charlene turned to face him. "She's coming here? In the middle of a workday?"

"Yep, she's taking a few hours off. She wants to see the guys jam. Got all excited when I told her they were with me. We're meeting with that songwriter today and we figured we'd bring him out here rather than to the lake house." Wade frowned, staring off into the distance. "I don't need any glitzy city slicker trying to tell me how to write my songs. He's in a metal band. Well, probably not metal. Hard rock. But how the hell can you tell the difference nowadays? It all sounds like noise."

Now that she knew they were alone, she felt more relaxed about sliding her hands up his chest. He'd gone all tense and definitely needed some soothing, though she wasn't entirely sure why. "So why are you working with him if his music doesn't suit you?"

"Sometimes you don't have a choice. You gotta play the hand you're dealt."

She stepped back. "You're telling me that?"

He didn't let her get far before he tugged her right back again. "It's complicated. My record company wants me to work with some new blood. They think my songwriting's getting stale and they're seeing a lot of success with crossover artists. They want my sound to be more rock-influenced on the next album."

"And you don't want that?"

"I'd want it a hell of a lot more if it had been my idea."

"So make it work for you. The Wade I used to know liked all kinds of music. The CDs in your truck cover a wide spectrum."

"Yeah. You're right." His jaw locked and she had to smother the impulse to kiss away the strain and try to prod him into sharing more about the situation. It was one thing to have a hot and heavy affair—hell, even to renew their friendship. They hadn't even had to try in that arena. It had blossomed again as if it had been in a holding pattern all the years in between. But she had to be careful how much emotion she put on the line. She had to keep part of herself separate if she hoped to get through him walking away.

Holding back hurt, but it was the only way.

"Maybe you're right," he said after a moment. "I haven't been giving this guy a fair shot and I haven't even met him in person yet. Better to keep an open mind." At the screech of tires on asphalt, he winced. "Here comes Hollie and from the way she's driving that sports car of hers, she's pissed. God help us all."

Charlene moved back and smoothed her hand down her hip. Hollie always drove her little fire engine red coupe like a woman possessed, but today she accelerated into the driveway like she was in the Indy 500. "Uh, did you happen to already tell her that you and I are—"

Hollie climbed out of the driver's side, seemingly oblivious to the cloud of dust she'd kicked up in the car's wake. She slapped an arm on the top of the car. "You gotta be freaking kidding me."

"I hinted. Guess she figured it out," Wade said under his breath.

Charlene was about to reply when the passenger door opened and a long pair of legs clad in gray Armani pants unfolded themselves from the tight confines of the car. But the fancy alligator shoes were a dead giveaway.

"Uh-oh," she muttered. "Bennett, we have a problem."

Rafe climbed out and shut the door, his bearing much more composed than Hollie's. But that was just for appearances. Even from the porch, Charlene could tell her brother was doing a slow burn. "What are you doing here?" she asked, trying for nonchalance. "I thought you were with mama."

"Why would you think that? And don't change the subject." Rafe ascended the porch steps two at a time. "I want to know what it is you think you're doing with my sister, Bennett."

Wade crossed his arms across his chest and cocked his brow, insolence written in every line of his face. Charlene was pretty sure that wasn't the best approach, but far be it for her to get in the middle of two stubborn men. Especially two stubborn men who used to be best friends.

"Is that a question, Rafael? Because if it is, I should ask how detailed of an answer you're lookin' for first."

"Wade," Charlene said, shaking her head.

"You better watch your mouth, boy. Don't think I'm afraid to touch you because you're made of gold now." Rafe bunched his hands into fists. He'd fought MMA for a while back in his teens, along with playing football, and she recognized his fighting stance when she saw it.

Wade, however, must've slapped on some blinders.

"Actually, I've been platinum—"

Rafe shot across the porch to nail Wade in the jaw, barely giving Charlene enough time to jump out of the way. Sure she was seeing things, she closed her eyes and opened them to find the two jerkoffs engaged in actual hand-to-hand combat, rolling across the porch floor while Hollie called out bets from the top of the stairs.

"For God's sake. Rafe. Wade. Stop it. Help me," Charlene called to Hollie. "Your brother's meeting with a songwriter today. He has to be able to talk."

"Oh dammit. Ruin a girl's fun, why don't you?" Hollie put two fingers in her mouth and whistled loudly enough to break Charlene's eardrums. But it worked.

The jerkoffs stopped whaling on each other and stared.

"Get the hell up," Charlene said, grabbing her brother's shoulder and pulling him to his feet. He might've started the fight but he'd clearly taken a few hits of his own. His mouth was bleeding, for pity's sake. "Really, Rafe? How old are you? Rolling around the floor in a frigging designer suit."

"Get off me." He nudged Charlene back and wiped his mouth before holding a hand out to Wade, who was resting on his elbows and looking mildly stunned. That didn't reduce the murderous gleam in his eyes. "Come on. Get up, you bastard."

Because Charlene saw that gleam all too well, she stepped between them before Wade could grab Rafe's hand and start the fight all over again. "Enough," she said sternly, planting one palm on her hip and extending the other to her lover. "On your feet before that songwriter gets here and finds you a bloody mess."

"I'm not bleeding," Wade said, reaching up to slap at the trickle from a cut beneath his eye. Seeing the blood on his fingers made him sigh. "Dammit. Pussy-ass fighter, always dealing flesh wounds."

"Don't test me, Bennett. Your hair's long enough to clean this porch."

"Yeah, and that patchy scruff on your chin could use some filling in. Want to borrow some of my testosterone?"

"Oooh, burn," Hollie said, laughing.

Charlene narrowed her eyes. "All three of you, enough. This is ridiculous." She wiggled her fingers at Wade and he took her hand, tugging her down into his lap instead of allowing her to help him to his feet. When she would've protested, he crushed his sinful mouth to hers and kissed the breath right out of her. "Fighting always makes me hot," he said as she pulled back to glare at him.

He *was* hot, no doubt about it. He was also a first-class ass.

Rafe let out a colorful stream of Spanish. "You could have anyone. Why my sister? I thought she meant something to you once." He shook his head, obviously disgusted. "Something else I was wrong about."

"Your sister's the only one I ever wanted," Wade said quietly, tightening his hold on Charlene and stilling her attempts to sidle away. "If you think I'd miss my chance with her now, you're insane. Both of you are," he said, angling his head to include Hollie.

Rafe crossed his arms across his broad chest. His tie was flung over his shoulder but he hadn't seemed to notice yet. "So you're staying put in town then? If you're going to ruin her reputation, the least you can do is stick around to help her salvage it."

"Dammit, Rafe. This isn't the 1600s." Never mind that she'd been thinking a variation of the same damn thing on her way over.

Also never mind that her heart was beating triple time and she couldn't seem to take a full breath. Had any man ever said they wanted her with that husky tone in their voice before?

No. Absolutely not. Only Wade. Whether it was a pretty lie or sterling truth, she was having a hard time not turning around and kissing him again, even with their company.

"So the answer is no then." Rafe shook his head. "This is exactly why I steered clear of you this week, Char. After the display you two put on at the drive-in, it was pretty obvious what was going on and I didn't want to get into it with you. But if you make it my business, then I need to call it like I see it. This has disaster written all over it."

Charlene shot Wade a glance under her lashes. So apparently they *had* been observed at the movies. They hadn't exactly tried that hard to be circumspect. She was just surprised she hadn't noticed anyone gossiping all week long, though she'd been wrapped pretty tight in her own thoughts.

Sometimes working her ass off had its perks. She'd been too busy to pay any mind to the rumor mill.

"Gossiping with my sister is making it your business, hmm?" Wade asked mildly, rubbing Charlene's hip in slow circles. Not to seduce, but to soothe. Funny how quickly they both moved to make gestures like that.

Twelve years apart had somehow turned into the equivalent of twelve minutes when she wasn't looking.

When Rafe didn't respond, Wade lifted an eyebrow. "Holl? Why is he here?"

Hollie heaved out a breath. "Ask him. I'm going out back to see the guys." Before anyone could say anything else, she hurried down the stairs and headed around the side of the house.

"I've been doing a lot of work at the library," Rafe said into the silence. "I happened to be talking to Hollie when your call came in."

"What kind of work?" Charlene asked.

"Research. What else would I be doing at the library?"

"Good question, since I'm pretty sure you have internet access in that cave you call your office at the architecture firm." Charlene stood and dusted off the back of her skirt as Wade rose to stand beside her. "Mama went over there to bring you lunch and where were you? Snugged up with Hollie."

She'd said it as a joke—Hollie spent way more time with her books than men, and Rafe wasn't her type anyway—but Rafe narrowed his eyes. "You're a fine one to talk about snugging up."

"Maybe you should try it," Wade said, patting Rafe's stomach as he passed by him. "Seems like you could use some decompression."

"That so? How would you feel if I *decompressed* with your sister?"

Wade stopped at the top of the stairs. "We better be talking hypotheticals here."

A dark car pulled into the driveway, cutting off Rafe's chance to respond. If he'd intended to respond at all. A tall, lean, dark-haired guy climbed out of the driver's side, and out of the passenger side popped a tiny brunette woman wearing platform boots, tight jeans and a V-necked shirt that showed off her serious curves. "Hi," she called. "I'm Jazz and this is Gray."

Gray pushed his sunglasses on his head and smiled as he rounded the hood of the car. "As advertised," he said, sticking a hand out to Wade once they met at the bottom of the stairs.

"Nice to meet you," Wade said, his voice sounding only slightly strained. "I'm Wade Bennett, and this here's Charlene and Rafe Martinez, old friends of mine."

Charlene tried to keep her smile in place. *Old friend.* Right. Well, she was, wasn't she? She would be his friend even when she was no longer his lover. "Hi there." She came down the steps to stand beside Wade. The cut on his cheek was still bleeding, but Gray and Jazz appeared to be ignoring it. Perhaps that wasn't all that foreign of a sight in California. "So y'all are from LA?" she asked when no one else moved to speak.

"Close enough." Jazz slipped her arm through Gray's and shielded her eyes with the side of her hand. "I thought it was hot in Cali but this is crazy. How do you even wear clothes here?"

Charlene grinned and gestured to herself. "Lots of dresses, but yeah. Stripping down is never a bad thing."

Gray waggled his brows. "Hmm, maybe we should move here, babe."

Jazz rolled her eyes and pulled on the end of her ponytail. "Ha. Nice try. Too much humidity for this hair." She bit her lip. "So, umm, could I trouble you all for a drink? We've been on the road forever."

"Sure thing, come on." Charlene motioned for Jazz to follow her back up the stairs. "You guys go take care of business and we'll get some refreshments."

"You sure you're okay?" Wade asked.

"We're fine. Go do your thing." Charlene glanced at Rafe. "You coming or going?"

Without another word, Rafe headed down the steps and trailed Gray and Wade out back.

"Ouch. Bad juju there." Jazz smiled. "He's hot though."

"My brother," Charlene said with a sigh.

"Ah. Not that I'm in the market for a hot guy anyway. I have my own."

"Lucky girl." Charlene smiled. With one glimpse, she'd guess Gray was the more serious, intense half of the couple. The girl practically bounced as she walked.

"What would you like to drink?" Charlene asked, leading the way through the front door and back to the kitchen. She stuck her head in the refrigerator. "Looks like there's soda, OJ and fresh lemonade. Unless you'd like a beer. It's five o'clock somewhere, right?"

"I hope so." Jazz laughed. "Lemonade for me, please. Don't want the kid turning into an alcoholic before birth."

Charlene took out the lemonade carafe and shut the door. "Kid? You're tiny." She cocked her head and squinted. She hadn't even noticed Jazz's baby bump at first glance. Then again, she had been pretty distracted. "Where is it hiding?"

Jazz laughed and patted her slightly rounded belly. "Bad enough I'll probably make him deaf. I play the drums," she said at Charlene's blank look. "In Oblivion. Gray's band? Well, it's not his band, but we're both in it. He's just doing a turn as a songwriter now since he polished up his skills while he was in rehab."

From babies to rehab in ten seconds. "Um, okay. That's good. Good to be productive," Charlene said, taking down a few glasses from the cupboard. It was handy that she'd spent so much time in this kitchen.

"Sorry. I tend to have diarrhea of the mouth. Plus I've been stuck in a car for hours, and I really want a nap."

Charlene handed Jazz the lemonade. "This is you set on sleepy? I'd hate to see wide awake."

"Yeah, I'm high-energy normally. Gray probably won't bring me with him all the time, but he's protective with the baby and all." Jazz sipped. "Damn. This is good lemonade."

Charlene nodded. "Yeah. My mother-in-law makes—" She broke off. *Not your mother-in-law anymore. And good thing.* "So Gray writes all the music for Oblivion?"

"No. Not by a longshot. Nick's too possessive for that to happen. The other lead guitarist," Jazz explained as Charlene filled glasses and set them on a tray. "Jeez, look at those sweet cowboy boots. They're pink."

Charlene looked down at her feet. She'd forgotten she'd chosen her favorite boots to go with today's outfit. "Yeah, I got these a few years ago. They're not the most practical for work but sometimes you just gotta."

"Where did you buy them? Somewhere around here? I need a pair before we go back. Pink's pretty much my signature color." Without waiting to be asked, Jazz picked up two of the filled glasses and tucked them in the crook of her arm. "Drummer," she said at Charlene's surprised glance. "I'm good at balancing stuff."

Charlene didn't immediately see the connection, but she'd go with it because Jazz was taking her mind off the tension between the guys. "I'm impressed. And yeah, the shop's near here. I'll give you the address before you head back."

"Perfect. Since Gray's working with a couple of country guys now, I figure I should broaden my fashion choices. Besides, they're hot."

They headed back through the house and out to the barn. "You're not really twelve, right?" Charlene asked, glad to hear Jazz snort out a laugh. "You just look super young to be having a kid. And married," she added, noticing the diamond on Jazz's hand.

"I'm not twelve. I'm even legal." Jazz grinned. "But yeah, we're getting a bit of an early start. Not early enough if you ask me. You can't stop love. Or you shouldn't."

Charlene adjusted her hold on the tray. The farther they walked, the easier it was to hear the ruckus out back. The Bennetts had cleared out one of the barns after they'd lost a horse last year and now used that one mostly for storage. Today it served as practice space. Melody's excited barking punctuated the rich male laughter and dueling guitars.

Then Wade's husky voice lifted above the noise, making Charlene stop dead. He sang one of her favorites, *On My Way Home*, and damn if her heart didn't ricochet from her chest to her belly and back again.

"You really think that's true? That you can't stop love," she said softly to Jazz. Wade's earlier comment about her being an "old friend" tried to rear its head yet again, but she'd be damned if she let it ruin her limited time with him. Hurtful or not, it was the truth.

Unless she tried to make them more than that—and for longer than two weeks. With every moment that passed, the more she wanted to try. There had to be a way to make it work.

"Absolutely. I could tell you some stories on that score. Suffice it to say, I'd never let anything stop me again. You only live once, you know?" Jazz sipped her lemonade and licked her top lip. "It's a bigger mistake not to go for the gold than to try and fail."

They walked around the side of the barn and she got her first look at Wade clutching a microphone while Glen, Jared and Gray jammed on their guitars. Rafe stood on the sidelines, looking sullen beside a hooting and clapping Hollie. Melody ran in frantic circles, her fluffy gold tail waving like a banner.

Wade finished the song and conversation erupted once again. Glen curled his tattooed arm around his guitar while Jared bent to speak in his ear. Gray dropped to a bale of hay and scribbled furiously in a notebook while Wade looked on.

"Your guy jumped right in," Charlene said.

"Yeah. He tends to do that where music's concerned. Hey honey," Jazz called as they approached. "How do you feel about me in cowboy boots?"

Gray looked up and pointed at Charlene's. "Like hers?" When Jazz nodded, he gave a thumbs up sign.

"Guess the boots are a go." Charlene grinned and hoisted her tray. "Refreshments, guys."

They were swarmed by the crew of thirsty men and Hollie, but it wasn't long before Wade pulled her against his side and grabbed his microphone again. "One more song," he told Gray. The other man nodded and gripped his notebook.

With a grin for Charlene, Wade launched into another of his hits, *Texas Girls*, and she had to fight to keep from winding herself around him like an eager kitten.

She'd never seen him sing live in front of an audience before. She'd been sorely tempted to go to one of his concerts—hell, she'd wanted to turn groupie and follow him around the country—but she hadn't been sure how she would react. Breaking down in tears or swooning wouldn't do her ego any favors. She was happy to say that at least right now, she couldn't stop smiling. It felt like he was singing for her alone, his deep, gravelly voice caressing the lyrics about sexy Texas women while he trained his dark blue eyes on her face. He rubbed her arm and she swayed with him, laughing as he pulled her into a modified Texas two-step.

Then she glanced up and saw Mr. and Mrs. Bennett standing in the mouth of the barn and forgot her steps.

"Keep going," he said against her ear, continuing the song with only the slightest hesitation.

Eyes on his, she did what he asked. Dancing with him and mouthing the lyrics she knew by heart eased her nerves. He was all that mattered. With his arm around her, she wouldn't falter.

By the time the song ended, Wade's parents had gone. Charlene tried not to let it bother her, but it was harder when Wade squeezed her arm and moved to speak to his band and Gray. Jazz and Hollie were doing their own Texas Two Step in the corner, and that would've brought back her smile if she hadn't happened to look Rafe's way.

She went to him and kicked his foot, making him grunt. "Don't you dare stand here and sulk. I'm an adult. I make my own choices."

"You think I don't know that?"

"Yeah, well, try giving me some support. Do you think I don't know this might cause me a helluva lot of pain? Of course I do. But God, I have to deal with Wade's family and whomever else might not agree with my decisions. Don't leave me hanging in the wind alone," she pleaded. "I need you and Mama on my side. Please."

He clenched his jaw. "I just worry."

"I know and I love you for it. But let me do the heavy lifting on that this time, okay?" She reached up to pat his chest. He was built like a bull and twice as stubborn. "You worry about you."

"I have room to worry about both of us," he said gruffly.

She couldn't help laughing. "Yeah, I bet. You concern yourself with finding a woman of your own, okay? You're alone too much and make *me* worry."

Something came into his eyes but he tugged her close before she had time to analyze it. "Do me a favor. Just one," he said against her hair.

"If I can."

"Just be happy, all right? For as long as you can, be happy."

She looked up at her brother and smiled as Wade's voice lifted above the others. "On it."

CHAPTER SIX

Wade's motto for life was pretty simple. When in doubt, have a beer with the guys. Since doubt was pretty much his constant companion lately, that motto certainly applied now.

For the past few days, he'd been working his fingers to the bone out at Coach's. In his downtime, he'd focused on his music. Gray had left him with a couple of really good songs, ones he actually thought fit his style while adding a new edge. They'd even spurred Wade to write like a fiend after Gray and his wife had gone back to California, and that hadn't happened in too long to remember.

Though that probably had as much to do with Wade's current source of inspiration as anything else. A source he'd be losing in a few days, unless he figured out one hell of a hat trick to keep her in his life.

But right now, he was going to talk and laugh and drink. Maybe even shoot some pool if the spirit moved him.

Sunday night at Pitchers meant no live band and an almost empty dance floor. Tinny music flowed out of the ancient jukebox and the crowd was much more low-key. As soon as Wade walked in, he saw Joel, Oakley, Carter Shaw, the town cop, and Jackson Brady—the championship team's star running back before he was suspended senior year for an "unfortunate indiscretion" as Wade's ma referred to it—at a large table in back. AJ and Randi were also in residence, though they sat at another table and appeared deep in conversation.

He didn't want to get deep into anything tonight but Charlene.

Smile in place, Wade headed over to the guys' table and slapped hands. He chose a seat at one end and settled in, listening with amusement as Joel and Oakley engaged in what he suspected was their usual trash talk.

Damn, he'd missed these guys. All of them.

Tucker Riley, an amazing NFL quarterback who was on a team that was surely Super Bowl-bound this year, came in a few minutes later and grabbed the seat between Wade and Jackson.

After a bit of small talk, Tucker pointed to the beer in front of them. "What's on tap?"

Jackson held up his glass. "It's Quinn, Tuck. What do you think is on tap?"

They laughed as they said "Bud" in unison.

Sadie came over with a fresh pitcher and a cold glass for Tucker. Sadie was only a bit older than them and had been the subject of more than a few teenage fantasies for the guys at the table. She'd been homecoming queen her senior year, which had only helped fuel the boys' hormone-ruled imaginations for most of their high school years. Sadie's family had run Pitchers for decades. "This one's on the house. It's damn good to see y'all in Quinn again. This town has been hurting for hot guys ever since you all left."

Oakley clutched his heart, pretending to take offense at her joke as Joel said, "Hey, take it easy there. A few of us at this table have been here all along."

Sadie laughed. "Oh, I'm perfectly aware of that."

Oakley leaned back in his chair. "You really know how to hurt the ones you love, Sadie."

"Is that what this feeling is?" she teased. "I thought it was indigestion."

Wade thanked Sadie for the beer and took a long sip. Yeah, it was good to be home. Even the beer tasted better. As difficult as the situation was with Charlene, and as much as he didn't want to talk to his brother once Colt returned home this week, Wade had to admit he'd needed this trip. He wished it had been under different circumstances for Coach's sake, but he hadn't realized exactly how desperately he needed a change of scenery until he'd arrived back in Quinn.

Jackson did the honors with everyone's glasses and they raised them, saluting Sadie. Sadie went back to the bar after winking at Joel and Oakley. Hmm, were there vibes pinging between the three of them or was he just imagining things?

It was probably his own hormone-addled state making him see things that weren't there. He'd heard some interesting rumors about some of the town residents over the years—Carter in particular was known to have some wild sexual tastes—but threesomes weren't exactly everyday occurrences in a place like Quinn.

In an attempt to drag his mind out of the gutter, Wade shifted toward Tucker. "You ready for this season? Everybody and their brother seem to think this is the year you take your team all the way to the Super Bowl."

Tuck offered up something about his teammates, deflecting Wade's praise as usual. He really was a humble guy, especially in light of all his accomplishments. Then Carter started talking about the best running backs in the NFL and Wade found himself pulled into a spirited debate.

A few minutes later, after agreeing to disagree and downing the better part of his beer, Wade clued into the conversation floating around the table. Jackson had a bit of a reputation as a hell-raiser, but he seemed determined to convince everyone he'd changed from the kid who'd been suspended before the big championship game for fooling around with a young female student teacher. It had been quite the scandal twelve years ago, but Wade figured that was old news.

His idea of old news and what some of the more conservative town members thought were two different things.

Wade leaned closer to Tuck. "What are you all talking about? That camp thing of Jackson's?"

Wade had heard a little about the ranch in Omaha that Jackson ran to help troubled youths learn cooperation and new skills and discover what it was like to have a sense of family. Talk around town was that Jackson wanted to start one in Quinn, and Wade thought that was a great idea. City kids could really benefit from coming to such a stable town and taking part in a different way of life. Plus, there were many local people who'd be happy to help assist with such a worthy program. And many who no longer lived there, like himself.

Jackson shook his head. "How the hell does everyone know about this?"

Joel grinned. "It's Quinn. News is rare so when it hits, it spreads like wildfire."

Tucker chuckled. "I think inviting Coach is a great idea."

Talk spread from there to comparisons between Tuck's coach and Coach Carr, and they all traded Coach stories for a while. They all worked their way through three pitchers, and by the time the last one was empty, Wade felt better than he had in a long time.

Only the hours he'd spent with Charlene could compete.

Suddenly Jackson rose from his chair and tossed money onto the table. "Hey guys, I gotta get going."

Just like that, he was gone.

"What's up with him?" Wade asked.

Tucker shrugged as Joel returned from the bar with yet another pitcher. A few of the guys got up to play a game of pool, and Wade debated joining them. Instead he relaxed in his chair and enjoyed a little people-watching while the conversation buzzed around him. Joel and Tucker talked about Lela, Tucker's ex-girlfriend—and current, if one listened to town scuttlebutt—for a few minutes, making Wade wonder if Charli was up-to-date on the Lela and Tuck situation. His girl barely had time to take a deep breath, let alone hang out with her girlfriends. His presence had really thrown a monkey wrench into her jam-packed life. She'd probably be relieved once he was no longer calling her for quickies and texting her dirty jokes and teasing questions.

And that thought was downright depressing.

Maybe he shouldn't call her once he finished here with the guys. He knew she had a yoga class but he'd hoped once that was over that she might want to engage in some naked R&R at the lake house. The days were unwinding faster than he'd expected and all he could think about was spending as much time inside her as possible.

He glanced up, tugged out of his thoughts by the sight of Mr. Riley shuffling their way. Tucker's dad already looked lit, and that was never a good sign.

Wade leaned closer to Tucker. "Hey, Tuck. Heads-up."

Tucker glanced at him, following Wade's gaze to his father. It was then that Wade realized all the other men had joined the game of pool or were placing bets, leaving him, Joel and Tuck alone at the table. Wade wondered if he should get up and give Tuck some privacy with his old man, then decided that was probably the worst possible idea. Mr. Riley had a bad history when it came to pushing the limits with alcohol, and if something went down tonight, he didn't want to leave Tuck to deal with the fallout alone.

From the way Joel stayed put, Wade could tell he felt the same.

Throughout Mr. Riley and Tuck's strained conversation, Wade struggled to keep quiet and stay seated. There were a couple times it seemed as if things would turn sour beyond just words. When the tense conversation ended with Sadie calling a cab for the clearly inebriated elder Riley, Wade breathed a sigh of relief. Tuck didn't need this kind of crap.

Not to mention, the uneasy conversation made him dwell too much on hard conversations he'd had to have himself—or would be having soon. No one had been drunk and no one had taken a swing, but his parents could wield icy silence almost as effectively as Mr. Riley had once used his fists on his son. The situation with Tuck's dad was beyond difficult, and Wade had trouble bearing witness.

Once Tucker's dad had shambled off and Tuck had said his goodbyes, Wade waved to everyone and made his own hasty exit. He had his phone out before he reached the parking lot. He'd had a bit too much to drink, so he really shouldn't drive. Walking to the lake house wasn't out of the question, but he really didn't feel like heading off on a long trek at this time of night.

He had a much better idea.

Rather than texting Charli, he called. She answered on the third ring, sounding breathless. "I just got out of class. I had a student stay late for some extra instruction."

"This isn't a co-ed class, is it?"

"No. But if it was?"

"If it was, I'd come down there and show the dude how to bend a whole different way for free."

She laughed. "You're terrible. You know, you should try a yoga class yourself. You carry way too much tension. I bet some of the deep breathing exercises would really help your mindset, not to mention your breathing itself. That could only benefit your voice."

"You got a problem with my voice, Charli?" he teased as he finally reached his truck.

"No, of course not. I'm just saying, it could be a good thing. You should come by next Thurs—" She broke off, clearly realizing he was supposed to be taking off by then. "Never mind."

"I'd love to take one of your classes," he said softly. She'd never guess how much.

"I'm sure." Her laughter sounded stilted now. "But if you really would like to try yoga, maybe I could get you a referral in Nashville. If you want."

Her attempt at nonchalance made him close his eyes. Did she have any clue how hard this was for him too? "I'm at Pitchers. I had some beers with the guys."

"I'll be there in fifteen."

"Wait. I'm not just calling because I'm not fully sober. I'm calling you because I'm missing you so hard that I want to break this phone in half just for being in the way. I'm not even gone yet and I'm missing you."

She made a noise that sounded suspiciously like a sob. His gut fisted and he tightened his hold on his cell as if it were her hand. He wouldn't let go until the last possible minute. "Then I guess we need to figure out how to make the morning not come," she whispered.

"I have a few ideas."

"I just bet you do." The huskiness in her tone brought a smile to his mouth, if only a fleeting one. "I have a few of my own."

"Do any of them involve extreme flexibility?"

"A good girl shouldn't encourage naughty behavior. Luckily I threw out my halo years ago when I decided it looked much better as a belt."

The laughter burst out of him, making a couple standing beside a nearby car turn and look. But he couldn't cut it off.

Charlene gave him everything he hadn't realized he needed—friendship and laughter, emotion and seduction. She was his past and his present, and damn if he didn't wish she could be his future as well.

"Well, far be it from me to try to change your mind. I'll be waiting for you. And darlin'," he murmured, "leave the panties at home."

Her soft exhale was the last thing he heard before she hung up.

She showed up fifteen minutes later on the dot. He slid into the passenger side of her little sedan and partially reclined his seat, then yanked her into his lap. "The car's still on," she reminded him as she wound her arms around his neck and slanted her mouth across his.

"I knew something was vibrating." He caught her laughter in her kiss and fisted both hands in her long, loose hair as his tongue slipped between her slick lips. They toyed with each other, bodies rubbing, mouths exacting a slow torment that didn't match the way she was grinding on his lap. He wasted no time in flipping up her short sundress to see what lurked beneath and let out a long groan as he found only damp, warm flesh. "Good girl. You please me."

"Oh, do I?" Breathless, she eased back, leaning against the dash while his fingers played out a secret melody between her legs. "God, Wade. Anyone could see," she said when the front door of Pitchers opened and a crowd poured out.

"Mmm-hmm. Does that mean you want me to stop?"

"No." She gripped his shoulders and rocked her hips into the insistent strokes of his fingers. "Absolutely not. I'm just saying that—oh shit, there's Carter."

The knock on the driver's window made Wade laugh rather than freeze. He leaned over and fumbled around on the steering wheel for the window controls and lowered the driver's side one with a grin. "Problem, Officer?" he asked, tongue firmly in cheek.

"Dammit, Wade, you know this ain't the place for…that," he said, gesturing to Charlene on his lap. And oh, the fact that Wade's fingers happened to still be moving in small, concentric circles on her clit under the folds of her skirt.

Not that she was complaining. She seemed to be too busy trying not to laugh. And gasp.

"I'm sorry, whatever do you mean? We're just catching up. You know, old friends and all."

"You need to get yourself under control, man," Carter said, glancing away.

Considering his tongue wanted nothing more than to be buried between Charli's silky thighs, he figured he was maintaining his control pretty damn well. But he nodded and sent Carter a smile as he slid his hand out from under Charlene's dress. "You know. You're right. This is completely improper behavior. I apologize." He lifted his wet fingers to his mouth. "Just let me clean up—"

"Wade," Charlene screeched, making Wade grin as his lips closed around the damp tips. Then he nearly groaned.

Fucking hell. She tasted like those peaches she smelled like, all sweet and juicy. His dick twitched. Okay, so maybe not the smartest idea.

"You're lucky I don't write you a citation, Bennett," Carter said, choking on a laugh.

"You're not on duty."

"Son, I'm an officer of the law regardless." He thumped the top of the car with his hand. "Move along, all right? I really don't think any of us need this to end up in the gossip column in tomorrow's paper, do you?"

Carter had a point.

"We're sorry and we're leaving," Charli said, tugging on a handful of Wade's hair until he laughed. And sucked on his fingers one more time. "You're incorrigible," she said under her breath.

"Make sure you do. I've seen some bare asses on patrol a few times, but I have no desire to see Bennett's. Damn boy is way too pale now that he's migrated to the city." Carter grinned and walked away, whistling.

"Well, that was interesting," Wade began, laughing again when Charli smacked him and scrambled off his lap to plop in the driver's seat. She put on her seatbelt with a defiant click. "You were worried that I wanted to hide. Guess you know now that I don't."

"There's not hiding and there's causing a scene," she said, putting the car in gear and shooting out of the parking lot with a squeal of tires.

He put his seat back into the upright position. "Huh. Learn something new every day. Here I thought I was being a gentleman by not pushing you back until your legs were around my neck and my mouth was where my fingers were." He shrugged and kicked out his long legs as much as he was able. "Guess I'll save that for later when you're tied up in my bed."

"You wouldn't—you're not serious."

Belatedly, he snapped on his seatbelt. "Hell yeah I am. I want to see you wrapped in ribbons and moonlight. And *only* ribbons and moonlight."

"I don't think a ribbon would hold me still for five seconds."

"It would if I told you not to move unless you wanted to be punished." He reached out and rubbed her thigh, noting how tense she'd become. "Unless you're not into that."

She gripped the wheel tighter and focused on the road. "Are *you* into that?"

He was tempted to defer and deny. The last thing he wanted to do was to make one of their remaining few nights together uncomfortable. But he also refused to stuff down any part of himself in her presence, especially when she'd nudged open this door last weekend. He'd been biding his time since then, waiting for the right moment for the next step.

This was as good as it was going to get.

"I like to push the limits," he said, his gaze intent on her face. Light from approaching headlights flashed over her, allowing him to glimpse the way she was biting her lower lip. Punishing it really, like he'd warned her he might punish her. "But I don't need it. I love making love with you, just as we have been. Feeling you break around me is the only thing I want."

She exhaled. "What if I panic?"

"Then I untie you. You know that. It's about exploring together, not forcing you somewhere you don't want to go." He kneaded her bunched muscles and she shuddered. "You can trust me, baby. I'll never do a damn thing to hurt you, unless you ask me to."

Her gaze shot to his. "Why would I do that?"

"Sometimes pleasure is sharper when it's mixed with pain. You won't know if it's that way for you until you try."

"Okay."

Her acquiescence was so sudden and resolute that he did a doubletake. "Okay?" he repeated.

"Yes." She let her lower lip pop free from the prison of her teeth. "I trust you with my life. I damn well can trust you with my body."

He clamped his hand around her thigh, waiting until he was certain he could speak. "Thank you."

"A dozen orgasms is welcome enough." Her smile was back, and he thanked God for it.

"You drive a hard bargain, Ms. Bennett," he said, lowering his voice intentionally on the last word. He needed to know if any part of her still identified with her married name before they stripped away the last boundaries between them.

"Martinez," she said back just as softly.

He nodded and let out the breath he hadn't realized he was holding as she pulled into the driveway of his rented lake house. From inside, he could already hear the manic barking. "She's going to need a run before we can settle in," he said, undoing his seatbelt. "You can take a bath if you'd like—"

"I'll run with you." She released her own seatbelt. "I have a lot of nervous energy."

"Good. Not that you're nervous," he said when she lifted a brow. "But more energy to burn is never a bad thing."

"Says you. I'm not tying you up," she mumbled, opening her door.

"You could. I wouldn't say no."

That earned him a surprised huff of breath. "Wade Bennett, you are a revelation."

He laughed as she climbed out of the car. He met her in front of the hood and took both of her hands, pulling her in for a quick kiss. "So are you, Charlene Martinez. In all the best ways."

"Carter didn't say anything about us fooling around. About you and me together."

"Nope, he didn't."

"He didn't even give us a dirty look. It was like we were any regular misbehaving couple. Not the most scandalous pair of people Quinn has ever known."

"Sorry, I think some other people took the scandalous crown first. Like Jackson. He won that contest years ago."

"He was a teenager when that stuff with Ms. Schneider went down. We're adults." She glanced out across the dark bowl of the lake, rippling with pale fingers of moonlight. "We're supposed to know better."

"If knowing better means I would've missed out on this, then call me stupid. Because nothing—hey, look at me," he said, brushing his knuckles over her cheek until her eyes lifted to his. "Nothing would be worth missing out on you or one second of this."

Her lips curved. "You always know just what to say, Strings."

"Yeah, well, remind me of that next time you get mad at me for back talking to Carter."

Her smile vanished, and he knew what she was thinking. *There won't be a next time.*

He led the way inside and they met a barking Melody just inside the front door. She jumped all over them, peppering them both with wet kisses that made Charlene giggle like a schoolgirl. Because Wade couldn't get enough of that sound, he debated playing with Melody until she fell asleep just to keep Charlene in that relaxed, carefree state of mind. He really didn't want her anxious. There were good nerves and bad, but he couldn't stomach seeing anything but contentment reflected in her eyes. Knowing she'd soon be beyond her fears didn't mitigate his discomfort at making her uneasy, even for a moment.

"We don't have to do this," he said when Melody trotted off to have a drink from her water bowl. He grasped Charlene's arm and found it covered with goose bumps. "In fact, if you wanted to be on top all night, I'd be just fine with that idea."

She gave him a mischievous grin. "Now who's chickening out? I'm curious. I want to see what you naughty musician types get up to in the big city." She started to move away, but his hold tightened on her arm. She looked back. "What?"

"I liked to be dominant in bed long before Nashville. You just never had reason to know." When her eyes flashed, he cursed under his breath. "Sorry. I'm just saying, I started pretty young. You knew me as affable Wade who sat around strumming his guitar. And that's me too, but I always had another side. One you can take or leave," he added. "No pressure."

She caressed his knuckles with her other hand, her face lifting to his. "I want all your sides," she said simply before walking away to summon Melody. A moment later, she opened the glass French doors that led to the deck and they went outside.

Once Wade could breathe through the constriction in his chest, he followed.

For half an hour, they threw sticks for Melody and chased her around the yard until her frenetic tail-thumping and exuberant barking lowered to a dull roar. Neighbors in Quinn were pretty tolerant, but a barking dog this late at night might cause some irritation so Wade did his best to wear Melody out. Not that it mattered if the neighbors pitched a fit. He'd be out of there soon enough.

Christ, he hated thinking about that.

Melody finally settled down on her plush pad in the living room and Charlene headed up to take a shower. He headed to the master bedroom and opened up the drapes to let in the moonlight, as was his habit. He'd only been there a short time, but he'd already developed a routine.

Already begun to build a life, again.

Not everything was as easy as meeting the guys at Pitchers and spending time with his girl. His mother had called him two days ago and asked him what the hell he was doing. His father had offered grim silence in response to Wade's attempts at contact. And Colt was on his way back to town, which meant that particular hell was about to break loose.

But the slice of heaven he'd stolen for himself made any price worth it.

He took the bondage rope he'd purchased the other day out of the drawer and tucked it under the pillow, just in case. He wouldn't nudge her anywhere she truly wasn't ready to go.

Charlene came into the bedroom, wrapped in a thick white towel that highlighted the rich glow of her skin and the dark hair that spilled like ink over her shoulders. In one hand she clutched her phone. "The girls wanted to get together for margaritas. Everyone's having man trouble."

He pulled on the chain on the lamp beside the bed. No way was he missing any details. "And you didn't want to commiserate?" he asked, turning down the bedspread.

She smiled, but it didn't reach her eyes. "My trouble is that no one can know I have a man."

"I'm pretty sure plenty of people know already." Suddenly too tired to remain on his feet, he took off his hat and sat on the edge of the bed. Not tired. Weary. He was so fucking weary. "We've already heard rumblings that some folks noticed us at the movies, and I've seen more than a few speculative glances. Difference is, I don't give a shit."

"Yeah, Lela's hinted around too, but she hasn't pressed. Juanita at the restaurant practically went cross-eyed when I told her. Paige is cool about it though. She's not too fond of Colt, so that might be part of it."

"Not fond of Colt? How can this be?"

"She thinks he's a pompous layabout. She also thinks it's ridiculous that a guy named Colt owns a horse training business. Said it proves he lacks imagination."

Wade couldn't help laughing. "More likely our mother's love of horses finally filtered down to him."

That still surprised the hell out of him. Colt had never been one for hands-on physical labor. Not to the extent needed to run that kind of business. Unless he passed most of the grunt work to his partner.

But he'd heard from Joel and Oakley that Colt had been taking his turn out at Coach's ranch with the rest of them without fail. Evidently, he'd changed some from when they were kids.

Then again, so had Wade. He'd hardened to the point that sometimes he thought the idealism that had driven him toward Nashville with a pocketful of dreams at seventeen had disappeared entirely. Then he looked at Charlene and that side of him came rushing back.

Dreams came in all kinds of forms. Figuring out which ones to chase was the tough part.

"Yeah, well, there's no convincing my bestie when she's determined not to be convinced." Charlene smiled and stepped between his legs, her fingers loosely gripping the knot of the towel between her breasts. "You turned on the light."

"I did. I want to see you. Us."

She stared down at him, her eyes heavy and dark under their fringe of black bangs. "Me too."

He rubbed her hip through the towel and inclined his chin toward the antique cheval mirror on a stand. "Turn that this way, would you, darlin'?"

She didn't hesitate. She crossed the room to the mirror and angled it toward the bed. Standing in front of it, facing away from him, she loosened the towel and let it puddle around her feet. Slowly, so slowly, she brushed her fingers through her hair, pushing the long, silky strands over her shoulders so they fell down her back. Below the ends her heart-shaped ass beckoned him, giving him no choice but to walk up behind her and kneel down. His palms already itched to cup her flesh.

He pressed his lips to the small of her back, tracing the dusting of freckles that fanned over her spine. Sliding downward, he sipped the droplets of water that still clung to her, following the curve of her bottom to the fullest part. He nipped her there before soothing the momentary pain with an open-mouthed kiss. He gave her other cheek the same treatment before murmuring, "Grip the sides of the mirror," and separating her thighs. "Watch me make you come."

Again she did as he asked without hesitation. She angled forward just enough for him to clearly make out the shadowy valley topped with a strip of dark hair between her legs. Below it her lips were puffy and glazed with need.

He couldn't wait a second longer.

Lowering his head, he lapped at her with one long stroke from her clit to her slippery entrance. She jolted, her spine going stiff until he placed his hand there and nudged her back down. She took his cue and widened her stance, pushing her ass ever so slightly at his face.

Not good enough.

He gripped her hips in both hands and plunged his face between her legs, absorbing her high, thin cry with a burst of masculine pride. Some petty part of him craved to hear her say it hadn't been like this with anyone else, that of all the ways he'd come in second best with his family and football and his career, that in this one thing—making her ache and then taking it away—he'd succeeded. He was the first. The only.

But he didn't say a word. He brought her higher with his lips and tongue and teeth, exploiting her excitement until she squirmed against him and made demanding noises low in her throat. Her clit swelled under his tongue and she grew slippery and oh-so-hot, driving him on to shove her that much closer to the pinnacle before he let her drop.

All it took was two fingers slipped inside her tight pussy for her to break. She vised around him, her cries turning to gasps as she ran out of air. Her hips bucked and she clamped down hard, holding him inside her while he fought to lap up every bit of what they'd created together.

Before he'd finished she whirled on him, fierce and beautiful with perspiration dotting her flushed cheeks and beading on the taut tips of her breasts. "You still want to tie me up?"

God, he wanted to grin. To laugh with her and then push inside her when her body was still shaking with amusement. But he knew this was a big moment for her—and for him too—and he didn't want her to think he didn't appreciate it. "Yes. If you want that too."

"Yes. I do." Without waiting for further instruction, she crossed to the bed and spread out on top of it, arranging herself on the sheets like a damn goddess. Then she parted her legs and gave him another glimpse of everything he'd just tasted.

He had to have more. *Everything.*

CHAPTER SEVEN

Charlene tried not to shiver as Wade stalked toward the bed. He was still fully dressed and she was naked, but that wasn't what turned her momentarily simmering lust up to a full-blown wildfire. His intentions gleamed in his eyes. He didn't have her captured in ribbons yet, but he bound her in place with his gaze.

She tried not to move as he tugged out red rope from under her pillow. *Rope*, for God's sake. As soon as it touched her skin, she realized it wasn't the usual kind they'd used at the Bennett farm or at Coach's ranch. This was smooth and silky, and she nearly purred aloud as he looped it around her wrist and attached it to the bedpost. "Too tight?" he asked, his voice strained.

"No. It feels good." His gaze shot to her face and she nearly asked him if he was okay. Perhaps he'd changed his mind—

She dropped her focus from his face to below his waist and she wanted to smack herself for being so clueless. He was turned on, not dismayed. Holy crap, was he turned on. At the sight of the visible outline of his erection jutting against his snug jeans, she licked her lips, causing him to groan.

"Don't do that or you'll make me take your mouth."

"Go ahead." She parted her lips intentionally, trying her hardest to break his control. Instead he moved to the other side of the bed and wrapped another length of rope around that wrist before attaching it to the bedpost.

"Okay?"

She felt a bit like a trussed-up turkey with her arms spread wide like that, but it wasn't frightening at all. Nothing he did to her could ever scare her. She trusted him too much.

Nodding, she stared up at him until he met her gaze. "I want you in my mouth." Even though she wasn't entirely sure how the logistics would go since she didn't have use of her hands. Even though she was aching again deep inside where only he could reach. "Please."

The word seemed to unleash something inside him. He placed one knee on the bed near her shoulders and fought to tug down his zipper. His low curses as he dragged the tight denim down would've made her laugh if anticipation hadn't stolen her breath. Again.

He pushed down his boxers and revealed his hard length. She barely had a second to appreciate his size and the darkness of the tip, crowned with a drop of pearly fluid, before he was straddling her chest and nudging against her closed mouth. A hint of his arousal seeped between her lips and she swallowed greedily, enjoying the flare of desire on his pinched features as she denied him entrance. Enjoyed even more as her supposed reluctance caused him to tap her cheek. "Let me in," he growled, and there was nothing polite about it.

Sweet Wade had finally been driven fully underground. And she wanted to rejoice.

She opened her mouth and he slid inside, not forcing her, not making her choke. He might be dominant, but he'd never take more from her than he was certain she wanted to give. She sucked him in, drawing hard on the tip, gauging from the way his face went slack that he liked what she was doing. Swirling her tongue around the head, she tried not to freak out at being so thoroughly pinned down by his big body looming over hers.

Relax. You're enjoying this.

Deliberately, she focused on the thick shaft she was sucking, and the way the cool air from the air conditioning felt on the oversensitized flesh between her legs. Her clit throbbed and she pressed her thighs together, whimpering at the pressure that wasn't quite enough. She flexed her wrists and worked her mouth, trying to get a better grip on him. He sank deeper and groaned, closing his eyes. The cords of his neck stood out in sharp relief as she teased and tasted, swallowing the quick pulses of fluid that bathed her tongue. Already he was close, just from going down on her and tying her up. The knowledge made her writhe beneath him and she tried to take in more of his cock, eager to help him reach the point of no return.

His eyes flickered open and he reached back to thumb her clit, making her moan. Gaze steady on her face, he slipped two fingers inside her, pumping them in and out while she hollowed her cheeks and tipped back her head, urging him to thrust.

"Oh damn, you are beautiful." He glanced over his shoulder and she knew he was studying their reflection in the mirror. She had to look wanton spread open like that while he fucked her mouth. Completely shameless.

Deliriously happy.

He rocked his hips, pushing deeper into her throat, and she narrowed her eyes on his face, needing to see every nuance while she fought not to gag. He took his time, forging farther while his fingers continued their onslaught. She closed her legs around his hand and he grunted and thumbed her clit roughly, giving her exactly the pressure she needed to get off. Sparks showered in front of her vision but she still saw his jaw constrict as she gave into the unrelenting tightening in her core. His fingers never stopped, ratcheting up the pleasure inside her. She whimpered and his pupils dilated, his cock giving a warning pulse in her mouth.

"You want me to keep going?" he asked, voice low. "Finish right there?"

She couldn't nod fast enough.

"Me too, baby. Me too. But I need this pussy too much." He slapped her clit just hard enough to trigger a new round of aftershocks. "You're going to get me wetter than your mouth did, aren't you?"

Nodding was all she was capable of. Even lying down, she felt dizzy and breathless. Her jaw was sore, her lips deliciously abused. When he pulled away, she gasped and turned her cheek into the pillow, helpless to fight the need to press her thighs together one more time.

"Let's see," he murmured, shifting positions. Then his mouth was on her again, his tongue invading her in one relentless sweep. "Mmm. More."

She shook her head, sure she'd reached her orgasm limit. At least for right now. His teeth scraped over her clit and proved her a liar. She rose off the mattress, straining at her bonds. She cried out again and again while he prolonged her torment, his mouth like a fever on her overheated flesh.

Without giving her a chance to recover, he stood and shed his clothes, giving her one hell of a peep show. Rippling muscles, tanned skin damp with exertion, a gorgeous thick cock. He rolled on a condom and straddled her again, rubbing his erection over her slit. Then he plunged.

Damn, her eyes practically rolled back in her head.

"Easy," he whispered against her mouth as he began to work her, sliding in and out of her in slow, deep strokes. Only when she registered his voice did she realize she was pulling against the ropes again, though curiously, she didn't feel chafed.

All she felt was cock. *His* cock. Stretching her open and making her burn in the most amazing way.

She rolled her hips up to meet his, desperate to participate. As hard as it was to keep her eyes open and on his, she tried to do it. She wanted to watch him come. To feel him explode inside her. If only that stupid piece of latex wasn't between them—

God, what was she thinking? She'd only had sex
without a condom one time and she'd gotten pregnant.
She'd told herself she'd never take a chance again, and
she'd kept that promise. Only Wade made her want to
break the rules. To test the boundaries.

To pretend that they weren't taking chances at all,
because this wasn't a temporary hookup. It was a real
relationship, and whatever happened, they both would
want.

"One more time," he grated, and she focused on his
glittering gaze. Tomorrow didn't matter. Just today. "Come
for me one more time."

Beyond speech, she shook her head. She squeezed
him, moaning every time he pulled out. She couldn't open
up enough for him, couldn't take him deep enough. He hit
her G-spot and she arched, tugging so hard on the silky
ropes that she nearly popped her shoulder out of joint. But
she didn't care because she was coming, her core
contracting as she flooded him with her release.

He crushed his lips to hers, stealing her gasps and
giving her his. Locked together, he drove into her again and
again, taking everything he needed from her body and
returning the pleasure tenfold. He turned his head and bit
the spot between her neck and shoulder, offering her that
extra jolt of pain while he dragged himself out and
slammed home one last time, reaching his orgasm with a
shout muffled against her skin.

When he slumped on top of her, his exhalations hot
against her neck, she had one regret. She wished she could
stroke his hair and cuddle him close. Forget spooning. She
wanted him to remain draped on top of her just like this for
the rest of eternity. Who needed to breathe?

"If that was pain, sign me up for more," she said
softly, smiling up at him. "I've never hurt so good."

His smile started slowly, a twitch at both corners of his
mouth. "I intended to paddle that toned ass of yours." He

braced a hand on the mattress to lift up his torso. "Didn't happen."

"No. But you freaking rocked my world in all possible ways."

"Ditto." He eyed the ropes and licked his luscious lips. "We'll save the spanking for next time."

Her smile froze in place, and she hated, absolutely hated, the pang in her gut.

He brought his gaze back to hers and shook his head. "We shouldn't have done this."

That she hated even more.

"Why?" she whispered. "Why shouldn't we? Afraid it was too good and now it's going to be harder for you to head on back to your groupies?"

Oh God, she hadn't meant to say that. Watching his face change as he registered her remark turned the twinge in her stomach into outright pain.

He pulled out of her and took care of the condom, then turned onto his side, facing away from her and the mirror. He was still breathing hard, his back rapidly rising and falling. And she couldn't even touch him while she apologized.

Not that he gave her a chance.

"It's not just about me," he said.

She stopped pulling futilely at the ropes he'd evidently forgotten all about. She let her arms go slack and tried to process that bit of woo-woo. Or at least it sounded like woo-woo, and possibly a kissing cousin to "it's not you, it's me."

Which flat-out equated to bullshit.

"Do you mind translating that for me?"

"It means that yes, my job makes things difficult, but there are always options."

Her throat threatened to close. She couldn't decide if what he was saying was a good thing or bad. Then again, what could be worse than him just walking away? "Are there? Like what?"

He shifted onto his back and blinked at the ropes. "Dang, you're still tied up."

"No kidding."

A hint of a smile touched his mouth before he sat up to free her. Once he had, he carefully rubbed each wrist, making sure she was okay. She half expected him to kiss the marks left behind. "Sorry. All right now?"

She nodded. "I'm fine. What options, Wade?"

After lying back down, he linked his hands behind his neck and stared up at the ceiling. "It takes both parties being willing to cooperate. It's not all just one."

"Really? Thank you for that sermon on how to conduct a relationship." She was having less trouble understanding him now. As someone who'd spent her whole life making concessions and waiting for the other shoe to drop for one reason or another, she heard his meaning loud and clear.

If she wanted to do all the heavy lifting, they didn't have to close the door on a relationship. As long as she didn't expect him to do anything other than maybe hold it open with his boot now and then.

She'd played that scenario once already. She and Colt had tried a long-distance thing for a short while after he'd gone to the NFL, but it hadn't taken long for them to realize it wasn't going to work. Waiting was always hardest on the one stuck home, living their ordinary life of laundry and paperwork and discount beer specials at Pitchers.

When Colt had come back to town, they'd had a reunion hookup of sorts. Her first and only one-night-stand—or at least that had been the plan. She'd been on the Pill so they'd foregone a condom, because she was young and stupid. So stupid. The repercussions from that night rippled to this very day.

And now Wade wanted her to wait around some more. If she kept the home fires burning while he chased glory, someday she might have someone to hold in the night instead of her phone. Except someday wasn't good enough. She'd been certain she would take any piece of him she could get, but the past week and a half had convinced her she couldn't. It was all or nothing with her and Wade. Anything less would break her heart.

"I'm not giving you a sermon on relationships. How the hell would I know how to have one? I've never had a girlfriend for more than a month."

She tugged up the sheet in spite of the warmth her body. She couldn't have this kind of conversation with the girls flying free. "I'm not exactly an expert either. Hello, divorced."

"You lasted five years. You tell me how the hell to do this right, because I don't have a clue. It's not like I don't have enough pressure from the record company. They're already on my back and now—"

"Now what?" she asked softly, gripping the sheet so she didn't haul off and hit him. She wouldn't be playing around either. "Now I'm just one more burden for you to have to deal with?"

When he didn't reply, she shook her head and swung her legs over the side of the bed. Her temper and his indecision were not a good match. Add in the leftover hormones buzzing through her and the crash from a pretty epic sexual experience and she was a hot mess.

Even so, a small voice inside her told her she wasn't handling this correctly. Of course he'd be stressed between coming up with new material for the new album and his creative clashes with his management. Then there were his notable family issues.

Of which she was a really big freaking cause.

"I didn't say that. I didn't think that either. Where are you going?" He grabbed her shoulder and she had to fight not to brush him off. His hand on her skin felt like one more wish she'd never see fulfilled. "You shouldn't be alone right now. You've never experienced anything like what we just did."

"What's that supposed to mean?" Indignantly, she whirled toward him. "You think I just sit home alone every night?"

"No, of course not. You indicated you'd never engaged in this kind of play before. Being bound is a bigger deal than you think."

"You're telling me that? I'm the one who just got untied."

He blew out a breath. "Dammit, Charli, I'm trying here. You're twisting my words."

"No, the problem is your words aren't enough. Colt and I tried the long-distance thing. I flew out to his games. I based my whole life around his schedule. If he could see me, I dropped everything to be at his side. If he couldn't—which was more often than not—I sat home and ate ice cream. It didn't take me long to realize I couldn't hack it, but he wasn't able to make any concessions so we broke up."

"Wasn't willing to, you mean."

She shrugged. "He was the star. I was the nobody. And you know what, that may be true. But dammit, I have a life. I can't keep putting it on hold for a day that may never come."

Except it already had. The time she'd spent with Wade had been the best days of her life, and it didn't much matter that she'd measured that time in hours not months. They'd experienced so much together. Not just sex. She'd gotten her best friend back.

Now she was going to lose him all over again.

Wade didn't say anything for so long that she began to wonder if he'd fallen asleep. Just as she was about to look back, he murmured, "I understand what you're saying."

"Do you?"

Tell me I'm wrong, that it won't just be me putting out all the effort. Tell me we can make this work. Tell me you love me enough to not want to let me go.

He didn't say any of those things. The bed shifted, and she turned her head in time to see him get to his feet. Being confronted with his very fine backside at the moment she was sure she was losing him seemed like a cruel twist of fate.

Worst of all, she didn't even care about his ass right then. She hurt too much.

"Yes." He bent to pick up his jeans. "I would never ask you to put your life on hold for me. I'm not Colt, Charli, and I hoped you already knew that. Guess not."

"I never said—"

"My entire life, I've been compared to him. He was bigger, stronger, faster. Smarter. More creative. Even in fucking kindergarten art class, I drew trees and he drew forests with fairies and frigging elves running between the trunks."

She nearly laughed. Under other circumstances, she would have. Not now, when his voice sounded so constricted that she wondered how he managed to speak at all.

"I dealt with all of that though. Because he really was better. It made sense that my parents thought so much more highly of him. The only reason I skipped a grade and he didn't was because he wanted to stay with his friends. Back then I didn't *have* any friends to lose."

She pressed her fists into the mattress. "Wade—"

"Don't. Let me finish. I could handle all of that. As I got older, I had my music, and he wasn't into that sort of thing so it stayed mine. No competition there. You and Rafe came to town, and the three of us were so tight that even if I hadn't another friend in the world, I would've had enough."

Her eyes smarted and she searched for a response. What could she say?

"I had my teammates too. I was happy to be the kicker. It's an important job. Tucker and Colt and Jackson could take the glory. But you know what I couldn't take? Look at me."

She looked, because she couldn't bear to face the other direction a moment longer.

He yanked up his boxers and his jeans. "I couldn't take our friendship being tainted by my bitterness when you fell for him. I know you had feelings for me too, twisted up ones of gratitude and our bond and maybe some chemistry too. You and Rafe appreciated—"

"Oh hell no. Don't you try to turn this into the fatherless transplant kids being grateful to make a new friend. What developed between us was so much more. It wasn't a big deal that our mother worked all night, because we could go home with you. You didn't pity us for losing our dad so young, you just loaned us your family." At his silence, she hissed out a breath. "You know why I fell for Colt? Because he made his intentions clear. He didn't keep me firmly locked in the friend zone for years then decide to kiss me like he loved me when it was too late for either of us to do anything about it."

Wade tugged up his zipper. "I was saying goodbye."

"The hell you were. What did you expect me to do?"

"You know what I expected?" His head lifted and his stormy blue eyes narrowed. "I expected you to choose him. Everyone else always did."

She jerked to her feet and headed to the chair in the corner where she'd left her clothes before her shower. She wasn't going to sit there naked when he clearly couldn't get dressed fast enough. "You never gave me the option."

"Yes, I did. That kiss was the option." He tugged his shirt over his head. "I think it was pretty fucking clear how I felt about you after that, Charlene."

She pulled on her sundress, belatedly remembering she'd forgotten her bra. She shoved it in her purse. "To you, maybe. You didn't even give me a chance to think before you were gone."

"Yeah, well, maybe if you had to think that hard, you shouldn't have been thinking about me at all."

Whirling to face him, she put her hands on her hips. "Or maybe this is just history repeating itself, except this time you tied me to your freaking bed before you hit the road."

They glared at each other, both breathing hard. The moment stretched out, and Charlene wanted to laugh at the absurdity of it all. She opened her mouth, prepared to ask him to back up so they could start this conversation again. They were both letting their tempers rule their brains, and nothing good ever came out of that.

"You've made it obvious where you stand," he said quietly. "And I'm standing way over here."

She nearly staggered from the finality in his voice. Well then. Guess there was no need to start the conversation over, because they'd gotten exactly where they needed to go.

"I suppose you're right." She crossed her arms over her chest. "Can you take me home now, please?"

Nodding, he picked up his hat off the nightstand. He put it on, then pried his keys out of his pocket. He was moving slowly enough that she wanted to scream with frustration.

If he wanted this over, it was over.

Throughout the drive home, both remained silent. He asked her again if she was okay and wished her a pleasant night. *Pleasant.* She would've snorted at that if she hadn't been so close to tears.

She didn't know if she would hear from him again. As far as she knew, he was still leaving on Thursday, but that was coming up quick. He sure as hell hadn't given her an indication whether or not he intended to contact her.

Figured that the first night she allowed someone to tie her up, they set her free.

The next morning she headed to work right after the first light. She hadn't gotten much sleep—okay, any—and didn't think that would be changing anytime soon, so she didn't see the point in lying around any longer. Not when there was plenty of work waiting for her. Always plenty of work. That was why she couldn't have a life outside of it. How could she travel and go to shows and play the country star's girlfriend when she spent most of her week chained to the counter at the store or behind the hostess's stand at Rosa's?

At least she had more flexibility with her yoga class. But even if she quit the studio, that only freed up a few hours a week. Why bother?

He hadn't asked her to be his girlfriend anyway. All he'd done was act like it was her fault that they hadn't become a couple sooner. Even if she had picked up on his confusing cues years ago, she still had to work. She still wanted—needed—that firm base of home and friendship in Quinn. Her personality and her lifestyle just weren't conducive to a long-distance relationship.

God, why hadn't he just *asked*?

For the next two days, she worked twice as hard as usual. The harder she worked, the easier it was not to pay attention to her silent phone. Ha, there was a lie. She couldn't *stop* paying attention to it. But she tried.

She also tried to talk to her mama at the restaurant Tuesday night, but it was slammed. Perhaps it was better if she never got to have the talk with her mother about what she'd said to Wade in high school. It wasn't as if she didn't understand how her mama thought. She'd wanted her only daughter to have security. To never have to be concerned for her financial welfare. Even if Charlene didn't agree with her mother's methods or her worry that her daughter couldn't fend for herself, she couldn't fault the basic desire behind all the rest. Her mama had said what she had out of love, however misguided.

Maybe that, too, should be left in the past.

Wednesday morning, she parked behind the feed store in her usual spot, then dug through her purse for the key ring that held the building keys as she walked to the side entrance. Paige hadn't arrived yet, which meant she'd have plenty of time to—

"What the hell are you thinking, woman?"

Colt. As if her week didn't suck enough already. Lord help her.

She stopped walking, head still down, fingers clutching the keys at the bottom of her purse. Her mind reeled while she flailed around for a response.

But he wasn't done.

"Is it our divorce? Was it harder on you than I realized? I thought you were adjusting well, but maybe I missed the signs." Shocked into silence, she looked up in time to see Colt push a hand through his dark hair.

"Say what?" She withdrew her keys, then gripped them to have some place to channel her anger. In a minute, her knuckles would be throbbing from the tightness of her hold. "You think me and Wade are all about you?"

He frowned. "Well, it seems logical to assume—"

"He kissed me back in high school, Colt. Are you forgetting that?" The look of shock that telegraphed across her ex's face made her shake her head. "Guess that answers the question if you knew," she muttered.

"You kissed him? When? Why?"

"The day he was leaving town, he kissed me."

"A goodbye kiss isn't—"

"Trust me, that was more of a hello than a goodbye. He just didn't follow it up with anything. I think he expected me to make the next move."

"You were dating me," Colt said, gritting his teeth. "Or have you forgotten that?"

"No, of course not. I didn't know he was going to kiss me."

"You could have stopped him."

"You're right. I could have. I also could have told you to go fly a kite when you asked me to be your intermediary with him two weeks ago, but I didn't." She sagged against the side of the building and shut her eyes. "It feels like I've been tugged between you forever, except I really haven't." *Because there's never truly been a contest.*

"What's that supposed to mean? And why didn't you tell me no if you didn't want to get involved? I had no clue you had anything personal left between you."

"You had no clue because you never paid attention. I'm just realizing now how little you paid to us."

Colt had never picked up on any of the vibes between her and Wade back in school. Not because he'd tried to pretend they didn't exist, he simply hadn't noticed.

All at once, everything Wade had said Sunday night came rushing back. His coming in second-best to Colt all his life. Being content to stay in the shadows, because he felt that was his role to play.

His needing her to prove to him that she wasn't the same as everyone else—that for once, someone had put Wade first.

Oh, he hadn't said that in so many words, and she probably wouldn't have been able to hear them even if he had. Not right then. She'd been too churned-up. Too emotional and too frustrated by the entire situation. Being in love with a man she couldn't truly have hurt like hell.

God, she was so in love with Wade.

"Have you seen him in the past twelve years?"

The indignance in Colt's voice only made her more tired. "Only at family functions. I haven't talked to him beyond that. After our divorce, he sent me a Christmas card with his phone number. I didn't use it until two weeks ago."

"And then you hopped right into bed with him."

Recalling that afternoon in Coach's kitchen nearly made her smile—and blush—until she took note of the way Colt was looming over her. "There was no hopping."

"Whatever. You're not the person I thought you were, Char. You could've at least told me first."

"Did you tell me first when you started boinking that snow bunny from Aspen who came here on vacation about two minutes after our divorce papers were signed?" she demanded.

At least he had the decency to look chagrined. "That was...a unique situation."

"Sure it was. As unique as all the other babes you've taken to bed since. And I haven't said one word. You know why? Because we're divorced. You chose that path, not me. I probably would've stayed in the marriage for the rest of my life."

God, wasn't that depressing. She would've spent the rest of her years wedded to a man she wasn't in love with. She loved Colt, like a friend. They'd had a lot of good times. But being *in* love was something else. Being in love kept you up all night, tossing and turning because you'd had a fight. Being in love meant hurting because he hurt. Because *you* hurt him, due to your own ginormous insecurities and your refusal to realize how bleak your life would be without him.

She was realizing it now.

It had been a little over forty-eight hours since she'd last seen Wade, last kissed or touched him, and her body felt like a block of ice despite the sweltering temperatures. Thanks to Colt, she was starting to melt—and not in a sexy way. Her old fire was returning, making it hard for her to remain there talking to him when she needed to be talking to Wade. She couldn't let him go back to Nashville without them clearing the air, and the clock was ticking.

Colt crossed his arms. "You're telling me you would've stayed married to me even though you had some kind of feelings for Wade all along?"

"I didn't say I had feelings for Wade all along."

"No, but your face did. If that's true, you sure as hell had some restraint all those years. Why didn't you tell me? Why didn't you tell him, for God's sake?" He shook his head. "Here I thought I was the only one who wasn't happy, and all along you were pining for my brother. My own frigging brother."

Biting her lip, she stared hard at the ground. "I tried to pretend I didn't feel what I felt. Until that kiss, he never gave me much of a sign that I was anything to him but a friend. Then he was gone. And you were too, not long after. We broke up not long after you went to the NFL, in case you've forgotten."

"I remember very well. Then I came back. If I hadn't knocked you up after I returned, we wouldn't have ever gotten married and you could've contacted him years ago to tell him he's a blazing moron for not making a move on you sooner." Colt heaved out a breath. "Jesus, how do things get so fucked up when people are only trying to do the right thing?"

Stunned into silence, she could only stare.

"Surprised you, huh?"

She nodded. Someday her ability to speak would return, she was almost certain.

"I chalked it up to you wanting an exciting fling with the music star. I tried to write it off as that. But while we've been talking, everything I ignored in school came flooding back. Seeing the two of you with your heads bent together in the library, laughing over who knows what. Listening to him talk on the phone for hours, only to find out he'd been talking to you. The way he wouldn't share his songs with anyone until you heard them first. I didn't pay attention, but it was all right there. It never occurred to me that for once, I might be second choice." He sighed. "Christ, I'm a cocky bastard. No wonder he hasn't spoken to me for over a decade."

She blinked, trying to stave off the tears prickling behind her eyes. But they didn't dissipate. "We fought. He's going back to Nashville and it's over."

"Why?"

For the last couple of days, she'd tried to puzzle that out herself. How had such a perfect night gone so wrong so fast? She'd finally reached the right conclusion—she hoped—thanks to Colt.

Somehow that figured, in an odd sort of way.

Wade had tried to tell her that relationships required both people to compromise. She knew that intellectually, but to her mind, that was his way of saying he refused to compromise at all. Then she'd compared him to Colt, just as he'd been compared to Colt his entire life.

No wonder he'd shut down.

"Because I wasn't brave enough to tell him I need him in my life, and I guess he needed to hear it."

Colt laughed and she jerked up her head to glare at him. He held up a hand. "No, wait. Don't kill me."

"I'm a woman on the edge here, Bennett, and you're not helping."

"I know that. I haven't helped you at all over the years. Yet another way I deluded myself." He looped an arm around her shoulders and led her to the low stone wall that surrounded the parking lot. "Do you think I was born stupid? Or maybe a football-related injury damaged my brain?"

It was her turn to laugh between sniffles. "Why do you say that?"

"I was in complete denial all these years. I've missed my brother so fucking much, and the answer why is right beside me. Here I thought he was jealous about my role on the championship team or my time in the NFL—"

"He was the one who made the kick that won the big game," Charlene interrupted, incredulous. "He's an amazing singer, with tons of fans. Why would he ever be jealous of you?"

"Ow." Colt rubbed his chest. "Direct hit."

She winced and hopped up to sit on the wall. Good thing she'd gotten to work so early. Paige wasn't due in yet and the store wouldn't open for a while. "Sorry. I'm just saying that he has a lot going for him in his own right."

"You're absolutely correct. But pompous asses who refuse to look at their own behavior wouldn't notice that as much, now would they?"

She smiled. "Paige thinks you're pompous."

"This isn't news to me. She's right. I just admitted it, didn't I?"

"You did." She smoothed her skirt over her thighs. "You're really not pissed that we're—that we—"

"All over town, from what I'm hearing?" When she blushed, he laughed and eased a hip onto the wall. "No. I'm not pissed. I love both of you, and from the sounds of things, it was long overdue."

"It really was." She sighed wistfully before she could stop herself. "But we should've told you first. We tried. We went out to the house to see you, but you were on your buying trip."

"Yeah. Came back with two gorgeous fillies instead of one, so it was worth it." He scraped a hand over his scruff. "I'm sorry I lit into you. I happened to hear some gossip down at Pitchers last night and I was up all night, thinking about it. Wondering how come my brother couldn't be bothered to call me but he had plenty of time to fool around with you."

She bumped his arm. "Sounds like you were the one who was jealous."

"Dang, it does, doesn't it?" He surprised her once more by grinning.

"A little bit. And he did call you, several times."

"I know, after I went to San Antonio. Never said my jealousy was rational." He peered down at her as she dabbed at her wet cheeks. "You're not going to let him just leave, are you?"

"No." She sucked in a breath and lifted her chin. "I'm not."

Now she just had to figure out how to convince him to make their forever a reality.

CHAPTER EIGHT

Wade moved a bale of hay out at Coach's ranch, smiling at the sound of Joel and Oakley razzing each other. He hadn't had a lot to smile about the past few days, but the camaraderie between the guys had definitely offered a few bright spots. He liked being back with his old teammates. Enjoyed listening to them hassle each other over the division of tasks and who was slacking and hell, even who'd eaten the last cookie off the tray of them that Lorelie had baked.

But all of that was about to come to an end. At least for now.

He stood to rub the ache in the small of his back. To make up for the fact he was leaving so soon, he'd been working his ass off the past couple of days. Not like he had much else to do with his time while he was in Quinn. His parents were talking to him, barely. Colt hadn't shown back up in town until last night, and they'd missed each other when Wade declined to go to Pitchers with the guys after a long day at Coach's. As much as he reveled in stories about their old high school glory days, his heart just wasn't in it. His heart wasn't in anything at the moment.

"You planning on doing something with that hay or you looking for a needle?"

Wade turned at Coach's voice and forced himself to smile. "Nah, actually, I'm about to cut out for the day."

"That so?" Coach looked at his watch. "You do realize it's not even seven a.m., right?"

"Yeah. I gotta head back today, Coach. My stuff's packed up in the truck already. I thought I'd get a head start on—"

"Running away? Yeah, I can see why you don't want to wait on that." Coach shook his head. "Boy, you never learn, do you?"

Wade tried to check his temper, but unfortunately it had been burning for days without an outlet. The backbreaking work had helped some. What he really needed was to have it out with Charli, but he feared if he started down that path, they'd end up on one of those TV talk shows, throwing chairs and whatnot. She'd always had a fiery personality, and in recent years, he'd developed one. His days of standing idly by were long over.

That didn't mean he wanted to fight with her. Not unless he knew for damn sure that they'd get to make up afterward. And right now, he didn't.

"It's not like you think," Wade said, pulling off his work gloves and tossing them aside. He would've preferred to not use gloves at all, but he was going into the studio as soon as he returned to Nashville and he couldn't chance something happening to his hands. Not when he had to play for the album.

His album, dammit. His backing band and studio musicians brought a lot to the table, but he needed to be part of every step. Luckily Gray had turned out to be easy to collaborate with. The songs he'd submitted for possible inclusion on Wade's album hadn't been set in stone. In fact, he'd encouraged Wade to put his own mark on them, and they'd spent a few hours on the phone since last week pulling them into shape. Gray had amazing talent, but Wade was determined the songs reflect his vision. It just so happened that Gray had no problem with that.

Now he had to head back and get the record company's stamp of approval on what they'd come up with before going into the studio. Coming back to Quinn had put him behind schedule, but he was determined to get the album done as fast and as well as possible.

He hadn't seen the last of Quinn, and Quinn hadn't seen the last of him.

Neither had Charlene Martinez.

"No? Then what is it?" Coach crossed his arms. "Enlighten me."

"I have a record to cut. I can't hide out here, no matter how much I may want to." Wade looked around the barn to save himself from having to meet Coach's all-too-knowing gaze. "I'm sorry I have to leave without doing more. I hate leaving the guys in the lurch. And you."

"Forget the damn work. We have enough hands here to take care of that. You boys have been right there to help me every step of the way. I half expect one of you to hand me the toilet paper when I stand up from the john."

Wade had to laugh. "No one told me that was in the job description, sorry."

"Good thing, because I'd have to backhand you. Bad enough I already want to for other reasons." Before Wade could evade it, Coach reached out to grip his shoulder. "What about Charlene?"

He braced. Simply couldn't help it. "What about her?"

"You plannin' on taking her with you? Or is this 'Wade runs away from home, the saga part two'?"

Wade shook him off and turned his back. He couldn't stand the censure in Coach's eyes. Not now or ever. One of the reasons he'd always stayed on the straight-and-narrow was so he could avoid this very look from one of the men he respected most. "This isn't my home anymore. I live in Nashville."

"Bullshit this isn't your home. You think home is just about a street address? It's about people who know and love you and won't hesitate to box you around the ears when you go off-track. Right now, you're so off-track you're in a whole new zip code."

"Charlene and I broke up, okay? You gave me the advice to go after her, and I did. We had an amazing time together, but it's over—"

"Did that amazing time include some alone time in my kitchen?"

Thinking he must've misheard him, Wade turned back. "Excuse me?"

"Don't pretend you don't know what I'm talking about. I raised a daughter. I know that guilty look as well I know my own face."

Oh God, his ears were going hot. If he was actually blushing, he'd kick his own ass. "I don't know what you're talking about."

"Let me remind you." Coach scratched his jaw and raised his gaze to the ceiling, as if he was thinking back. "A week ago last Saturday, Ms. Charlene brought over a picnic basket. You wandered outside half undressed and charmed her into…well, not bed, obviously, but—"

"Okay, okay. I got your point." Yes, he was blushing. No doubt about it. Shit, Coach was the second-best thing to his father. "Do you have a hidden camera in there or what?"

"Or what. The ranch hands stood outside giggling until it turned X-rated then some of them had the decency to get back to work." Coach shook his head. "Don't ever think I don't know what goes on here in Quinn, Wade. Especially on my own property. I have eyes and ears everywhere, and they all have big mouths."

Wade had to laugh. "No fucking kidding. Pardon me, sir," he said automatically.

It was Coach's turn to chuckle. "You're allowed to swear in my presence now. You're a grown man, are you not? Grown enough to defile my kitchen." Before Wade could apologize, Coach patted Wade's arm. "Don't worry. It wasn't the first time it was used for such purposes. I bet it won't be the last either."

Wade sputtered into silence. Yeah, there wasn't a whole lot he could say to that.

"So you're just heading back and that's it? You're done with work here and you're done with Charlene."

"No, it's not like that at all. I have to go back and start cutting my album. My record company booked a studio. I have to be there."

"But you'll have down time."

"I will. And I'll make the trip back here as soon as I'm able. I'm not leaving you all in the lurch. And of course, I'll help financially—"

"Do I look like I need your money?" Coach narrowed his eyes and angled his head, making Wade feel about six inches tall. "Another thing about people from back home. We'll bring you back down to size right quick if you get too big for your britches."

That phrase made Wade think of his first night with Charlene. He clamped a hand around the back of his neck, squeezing hard to relieve the tension. "Christ, Coach, I fucked it all up. I should've told her I wanted to make a commitment to her, not wait until she said it first. You're right. I'm a coward."

"It's damn easy to lose the words when you need them most if you've been burned before."

"But words are my business."

"No, words are the vehicle you use. Your business is making people feel things. And you can't make them feel what you won't let yourself feel in the first place." Coach kicked a bale of hay next to the wall and lowered himself onto it, indicating Wade should do the same. After Wade obliged him, Coach patted his shoulder. "You caught a raw deal with the situation with Colt, son."

"Which situation? The fact that everyone in town thought he was a hot commodity and I was the also-ran? Or the fact he married the girl I loved when I'd be surprised if he managed to tame his wandering eye during his marriage any better than he had beforehand?"

Guilt surged through Wade's chest. Shit, he shouldn't have said that. Shouldn't have thought it either. His brother was a good guy. Sure, he was a flirt and a charmer but that didn't mean he hadn't been faithful. Not even close.

One way or another, he had to deal with his bitterness before it poisoned everything it touched.

"Uh, not to put too fine a point on it, but your brother left the NFL after three seasons due to injury and now runs a horse training business. You, on the other hand, have how many hit singles and albums to your credit?"

"I don't keep track."

"Sure you don't." Coach expelled a long breath. "Look, no one's arguing that you've got some issues with your brother. You need to sort those out. They've been festering way too long."

"Tell me about it," Wade muttered.

Coach surprised him by smiling. "All siblings have their issues to work out. Comes with the territory. I always wished my girl had one or two of her own. But it wasn't meant to be."

"I'm sorry," Wade said, instantly chagrined. Here he was feeling sorry for himself regarding his brother, and Lorelie hadn't had the chance to have brothers or sisters because her mother had died in childbirth having her. Talk about selfish.

"Life's too short, Wade. Even the longest time is too short. My experience these past few weeks has brought that home to me more than ever." The older man clapped Wade on the back. "Don't make the same mistakes I did. I took way too long to propose to Lorelie's mother, and those were days I sure wished I had back at the end of her life. Time is the one commodity that can't be invested. You spend it now or lose it forever."

Wade swallowed over the tightness in his throat. "I'm not sure she feels about me the way I feel about her. I know she feels something, but—"

"That girl's been in love with you since she was cheerleading you boys on for the win."

Wade shot Coach a surprised glance. "You never told me that."

"It wasn't my place to tell you. You had to decide what you wanted to do with your life. I tried to nudge you toward her, but you gave up the field to Colt every time."

"So, what, I was supposed to fight for her like a piece of meat?"

"No. You were supposed to take a stand and tell her exactly what she means to you. There won't be a fight after that, because she's already yours. Problem is, then you have to be willing to do what's necessary to keep her."

"I'll do anything."

"Then stop sitting around here and go do it." Coach got to his feet. "Going long is another way to get the ball in the end zone, Wade, but it doesn't work so well as a relationship strategy."

"You're right. I need to get a touchdown once and for all."

"Just see to it you don't do it again in my kitchen." Grinning, Coach pulled him in for a quick hug. It pleased Wade to feel some of the other man's strength returning. "I'll see you again soon. Don't be a stranger."

"I won't. I'll be back before you know it."

"See that you are."

Wade let Coach get to the doorway before he called out to him. "Thank you. Again."

"You're welcome. Now make the championship-winning kick one more time and make me proud." With a final smile, Coach headed out into the bright sunshine.

Wade soon followed. He walked around saying goodbye to everyone, though there weren't many people there early on Wednesday in the middle of the work week. But he said goodbye to Joel and Oakley and a few others before rounding up Melody from where she was chasing rodents in the pasture and put her in the truck for the short drive to the feed store. Opening time was still a couple of hours away, but he knew Charlene tended to get an early start. Whereas he would've been happy to sleep until noon, and had done so many times since he'd gone to Nashville.

But things were changing now. His girl was an early riser, so he'd learn to deal with it too. He intended to help her out wherever he could so he could make her jobs easier. If she got done with work faster, maybe she could arrange more time off. And more time off meant they could build a life together.

He didn't have to be in Nashville full-time. In fact, he didn't even want to be. Texas wasn't next door but it wasn't another continent away either. If they tried, they could figure out a way to make it work.

A few minutes later, he swung into the near empty parking lot. Only one car was there—Charlene's. Perhaps his luck was changing. He smiled and pulled into a spot before getting out to head to the side entrance. She probably wouldn't be happy to be disturbed while on the job, but he hoped his proposition would sweeten the deal.

Halfway to the door, he stopped and blinked. Blinked again when the picture didn't change.

A few feet away, Charlene and Colt were sitting on the low wall that bordered the lot. Laughing. And hugging.

"Sorry to interrupt," Wade said coldly, ignoring the small voice in the back of his head warning him to shut the hell up and wait for the facts. Unfortunately, small voices were easily overrun by loud accusations. "I was hoping to catch Charlene alone, but I see I was too late."

They didn't break apart guiltily. Not even close. Colt eased back, his hand still on Charlene's lower back. "Brother, it's been a long time."

"That it has." Wade dragged his attention to Charlene's face, and her dark depthless eyes. Pain etched grooves around her mouth, and he hated that he'd caused some of those lines to exist. "I think it's long past time the three of us talked."

"Are we actually going to talk?" she asked quietly. "Or are you going to continue staring at us as if you caught us in bed together?"

Wade shut his eyes. He probably was doing that, but he couldn't help it. Seeing them wrapped in each other's arms, even as friends, caused too many memories to surface that he hadn't begun to deal with yet.

"No," he said, once he'd shoved his emotions back into line. He opened his eyes and focused on her face. Her beautiful, perfect face. "I'm going to tell you I love you, and that I want to marry you. And that because I'm a jackass, there's a very good chance I'm going to screw things up, just like I did the other night. But I'm going to be by your side to fix them every damn time, as long as you'll be patient with me and give me time to learn. We'll both make whatever compromises are necessary to make this work, I promise."

"Wade." She covered her mouth with her hand, her eyes filling. She jumped down off the wall and ran over to him, launching herself into his arms.

He caught her, cupping her head in his palm as he met his brother's eyes over her head. Colt was grinning a full-on, shit-eating grin.

"Hell yeah," Colt said. "About damn time."

Wade was so taken aback he almost missed what Charlene murmured against his chest. "Yes. The answer's always been yes. Even before you asked."

He tugged her back to frame her face between his hands. "You do realize this is kind of a small town scandal. As The Quinn Turns or some shit."

"You mean that I've been a Martinez then a Bennett then a Martinez and back to a Bennett again? But not the same Bennett?"

"Yeah, that about sums it up," Wade said wryly.

She sniffled. "Ask me if I care."

"She doesn't," Colt put in. "And I don't think you're giving the people of Quinn enough credit. All that time you've spent in the city must've colored your perception a bit. This is one heck of a town, and the people are more understanding than you think. Give them the chance to prove you wrong." He stepped down from the wall and crossed over to them. "Congratulations, man," he said, extending his hand to Wade.

Wade hesitated for less than a moment before slipping one arm away from Charlene to return Colt's handshake. His brother pulled him into a hard hug, and he hugged him back, surprised to feel his eyes go damp. "Damn, I've missed you," Wade said in an undertone, shocked that it was true.

"Me too." Colt sounded hoarse. "Me fucking too."

"Well now, this isn't the kind of scene a girl expects to see when she walks to work early one mornin'."

The three of them broke apart and turned toward the female voice.

"Paige," Charlene said, laughing. She gestured toward Wade. "I don't think you've met Wade yet."

"No, I have not, because you've squirreled him away." Slowly, she approached, her curvy hips swaying in a lime green dress with a plunging neckline. "Though I gotta say I understand why. That is some nut you got there, girlfriend. Hiya Wade," she said, wiggling her fingers.

"Hi." He couldn't help grinning in return before he turned his mouth against Charli's hair. "*She's* your best friend?"

"Yes." She glanced from Paige to him and back again. "Well, no."

"Pardon me? Just because you have two armfuls of man over here doesn't mean squat. Chicks before dicks, remember?"

Colt chuckled. "Paige, honey, you're over a decade too late. These two were best friends a long time ago, and I think they're picking up where they left off."

"Speaking of picking up," Wade began, lifting Charli into his arms. Her squeals only made him grin. "I have a proposal to do properly. We'd appreciate the witnesses, if you don't mind," he said over his shoulder.

Colt glanced at Paige. "You game?"

She lifted a brow. "The better question is, are *you* game?"

"Sure." He held out his arm, and she took it with obvious reluctance. "I'm always up for a party."

Wade carted a now-laughing Charli over to his truck. He pulled down the tailgate and set her on the edge of the flatbed before scrambling up beside her to grab his guitar case. Grabbing it, he jumped back down and set the case on the ground. He pulled out his guitar and got down on one knee.

"Shit. Forgot something." He popped up again to go over to the grass that ringed the parking lot while Colt made a phone call and Paige laughed. Charli just kept rocking back and forth like a kid waiting for cake.

Once he'd found what he was looking for, he carefully tucked it in his pocket and went back to the truck to kneel in front of Charli. He was seriously winging this, but hopefully she wouldn't mind.

"I call this song *To All Of Charli's Mistakes*."

"Now there's a proper wedding march," Paige said under her breath.

Charlene looked at him wide-eyed. "We're not married yet. Tread gently, Bennett."

Smiling, he strummed his guitar, setting off into an easy rhythm. This wasn't going to be his best song. As long as it made her laugh, it would be worth it. Her laughter was worth everything. He started to sing.

There once was a pretty girl

One day she met a boy and heard him sing a song.
She was sorry to say.
That he'd gotten the words all wrong.
She helped him get it right.
Then she told him her secret.
She wasn't perfect, not even a little bit.
But he didn't care, because her hair smelled like a
peach pit.

Laughter broke out around him. A crowd had started to form around them—workers at the store, perhaps, or early customers or maybe just gawkers, because word traveled fast in Quinn—but he focused only on Charlene's delighted grin.

So to pay her back for lighting up his life.
And agreeing to be his wife.
He wrote her a song about all her mistakes.
Which weren't too many and weren't too few.
Because they made me fall in love with you.

All had gone quiet except for Charli's soft exhalations as she struggled not to cry. He set down his guitar and pried the smushed purple flower he'd rescued out of his pocket. "This is only temporary, of course. Hand, please," he said.

Charli stuck out her trembling left hand, saying nothing as he fashioned the thin stem of the flower into a band around her finger. The bloom was a bit worse for wear, but it would do until—

"Oh fuck," she said when the stem snapped.

"Whoops. Guess we'll have to wait for the diamond." Wade laughed and tossed the pieces aside before dragging her into his arms. "Marry me," he said, his lips hovering over hers.

She grinned. "You bet your ass I will."

He crushed his mouth to hers, giving her one hell of a kiss. Whoops and cheers broke out around them, and as he moved back, he saw Lela and Tucker and a couple of their other friends clapping. Even Hollie and Rafe were in the assembled group, and they were smiling too. How had they gotten there so fast? Who had—

Then Wade glanced at his oh-so-smug brother. "How did you pull off getting them here?"

Colt dusted off his shoulders. "I have my ways. Also, it helped that a bunch of them were right down the street at The Lone Bean when I called. Got lucky. Like you did," he said with a grin, glancing from Wade to Charlene.

"Damn straight. Thank you."

"I'm happy for you two. I'm also happy that our friends got to share in your special moment. Since y'all don't seem to have a problem with openly sharing *other* special moments, I figured it fit." Colt chuckled at Wade's lifted eyebrow. "Congratulations, man."

"Thanks, bro. I mean it." After they shook hands one more time, Colt headed over to speak to their friends.

Wade dug out his phone. "Sorry, babe. I have an urgent call to make. One second."

He dialed his manager and waited until he got voice mail. "So Stanley, bad news. Well, bad news for you, great news for me. Turns out I'm getting married so I'll need to push my studio time back a bit. I promise to cover any extra costs incurred, and I'll also be recording one kickass album. I mean it, you and the suits are really going to love it. I'll be in touch once I'm back from my honeymoon." He clicked off and flashed a grin at Charli. "Well, look at that. Guess I'm in town a little longer."

Her lower lip quivered and it took everything inside him not to lean forward to bite it. "We're getting married now? This week?"

"That's up to you. I just wanted to get them off my back. They'll feed that to the piranhas in the tabloids and the record company will be thrilled because it'll get my name back in the news. Everything's a soundbite to them." He grimaced. "This is the life I'm bringing you into. I'm sorry."

She slid her arms around his waist. "Don't be sorry. It's yours, and I want to live it with you. I want you and everything that comes with you, good and bad."

"From now on, it's ours," he corrected, brushing his fingers over her cheek. "And now it's time for the hero to kiss the girl." He grinned. "Again."

EPILOGUE

Sun poured through the moonroof, and the music was pumping good, strong country, the kind that never failed to make Wade smile. Melody was camped out in the back seat and had her head stuck out the window.

And in his passenger seat sat the most beautiful girl he'd ever seen, wearing tiny shorts and a cleavage-revealing top that made him want to pledge fealty to the designer who had created tank tops with basically nonexistent shelf bras.

Charli had just schooled him about shelf bras the other day. He still hadn't lifted his jaw off the ground.

"Are you sure your record company's going to be okay with you taking two weeks off? And we didn't even get married yet. They're going to flip when they find out you still need to take a honeymoon." She sighed. "I'll have to beg, borrow and steal a vacation anyway, after these few days I'm taking now. We may have to just meet in the middle between Quinn and Nashville. We can always reserve a honeymoon suite at some classy hotel and fuck like bunnies."

"As much as I like that idea, both of your bosses are giving you two weeks off for our honeymoon, so suck it up, Martinez. I'm thinking September."

Her eyes flashed and he had to swallow a chuckle. "My mama is not my boss. Paige most definitely is not my boss either. We're partners. How do you know they're okay with September?"

"I talked to them both. I think your mama's a little sweet on me now."

Charlene huffed out a breath but a smile lurked in her eyes. Mrs. Martinez had even put Wade's picture up on the wall of her restaurant with some of her other favorite singers, so he knew he'd made progress there.

Slow and steady won the race, and he was making good time.

"Uh-huh. Well, at least, I'll be done teaching yoga next month, so we're good there. Maybe I'll pick up another class in a few months when things settle down."

Settle down. Yeah, right, like that was ever going to happen. He was grateful he'd gotten a chance to spend a couple of extra weeks in Quinn with Charlene and his family and Coach, especially after Coach overdid one day and gave them all a scare. He was glad he'd been around that day to help out.

Unfortunately, the time he'd taken off only meant he'd have to spend twice as long in the studio, when all he wanted to do right then was hang with his girl. They would be doing the long-distance thing for a while, and that wouldn't be easy. Not in the slightest.

But for the first time in a long time, he was excited about the songs he'd written—both with Gray, and on his own. He had half a mind to throw *All Of Charli's Mistakes* onto the setlist of the benefit show he was doing at a honkytonk outside of Nashville next week. Charli would get a kick out of it, and since that show would be the first one she'd be in the audience for, it would be doubly special.

"Then what's the problem?" he asked, toying with her hair. He couldn't keep his hands off of her. Forget tying *her* up—something they'd done twice more, with incredible results both times—he'd need to bind his own wrists to stop touching her.

She worried her thumb over her diamond and emerald engagement ring, a small smile playing across her mouth. "I guess there isn't one. How am I supposed to worry if my sexy fiancé keeps finding ways to calm me down?" Her voice turned husky. "September, huh? That's soon."

"Too soon?"

"No, September's perfect. Maybe by then your parents will agree to attend the ceremony."

"They're already halfway there. They'll come around. Colt's on his way to convincing them. He's a bulldog when he wants to be."

"That he is." She turned her head toward the window, smiling as the warm breeze lifted her hair. "He's being awesome about all of this."

"He sure is. I'm guessing he'll extract payment some point. Probably put us to work mucking out horse stalls at C&D," he said, laughing.

"At least we can count on him attending the ceremony, as strange as that may be." She sighed. "Not so sure about Rafe."

"He'll accept us eventually too." Wade was almost sure of it.

"Yeah, he does seem to be softening. Marginally. It helped when he found out you bought the Sutter place." Her lips curved. "I think he doubted the likelihood of you really committing to me until then. Still think he might skip our wedding, unless we give him another five years to get used to the idea."

"I was thinking destination wedding anyway. You, me and a JP. Possibly a random stranger or two for witnesses and/or your mama."

"Oh." The way her face lit up from within made his gut tighten and his throat close. "God, I love you. I'd suck you off right here if I wasn't afraid of getting my head caught under the steering wheel."

"Ditto." He laughed. "Well, not the sucking off part. Though another kind of vehicular sex could possibly be arranged…"

"Wait until we're out of this area. I saw a cop back there."

Ah, his little rule-abider. She'd never lose that side of herself entirely, but boy, did he enjoy tempting her to sin.

"So how do you feel about Aruba? White sand beaches, getting married by moonlight. Doing other things by moonlight."

"I say hell yes. You never cease to surprise me, Strings."

God, he loved when she used that nickname. Still. Always. "Good. I hope I always will."

"No doubt there. You keep me on my toes." Her smile turned sly. "And on my knees."

He gripped her thigh, slipping his pinky under the hem of her shorts while he drove. "Hang on, honey, I'm about to up my game."

Want to read more about Jackson and Wade?
Enjoy these excerpts from other Boys of Fall
books. Available now!

Out of Bounds
by Erin Nicholas

*As star running back for his high school team, Jackson
Brady led a charmed life—until the wild child pushed a
little too far. And thanks to snitching goody two-shoes
Annabelle Hartington, Jackson endured scandal, shame,
and suspension from the team before the championship
game. His ensuing downward spiral would have been far
worse if not for Nicholas Carr, his high school coach and
mentor.*

*Now, twelve years later, Jackson doesn't think twice
about returning to Quinn, Texas, to help out when Coach
suffers a heart attack. It's an opportunity to atone for past
sins and prove he's ready to give back to the close-knit
community. And he knows just the person to help him—
the same woman who brought him down all those years
ago. A respected and beloved teacher, if Annabelle is
willing to take a chance on him, everyone
will know Jackson's a new man.*

*But he's not the only one who's changed. Though she's
just as smart as he remembers, Annabelle is also sweet,
kind, loyal—and hiding a surprisingly passionate woman
behind her staid schoolteacher clothes. Suddenly proving
himself to the town might be more difficult than he'd
thought. Because while Jackson may have shed most of his
wild ways, turns out nothing stirs his inner bad boy quite
like Annabelle.*

Excerpt:

"Hi, Jackson."

Annabelle's soft voice behind him felt as if she'd stroked her hand down his arm. Every muscle in his arm and his stomach tightened. And maybe a couple a little lower.

From a simple "hi"?

That reaction definitely drew Jackson's attention from the conversation at the bar. It had been mostly small talk, a few questions about Coach, and him trying to nonchalantly feel people out about any land for sale. Not to mention trying, unsuccessfully, to work his desire to bring some of the city teens to Quinn into the conversation. He needed to know if Tom was the only one who was against the idea or if that was going to rile up everyone.

But the moment Annabelle said, "Hi, Jackson", he forgot about everything but wanting to know how her hair smelled. Again.

He turned to face her fully.

Damn, she looked good.

That was the thought that first hit him. And it was strange. She was wearing one of those full skirts again that didn't show a thing. But the image of her in yoga pants was branded on his brain and he could easily conjure it.

The memory made him grin. "Hey, Annabelle."

She took a deep breath and looked, if he wasn't mistaken, a little shy. "I was wondering if you'd dance with me."

Dance with her? Oh, really?

"I've never ever turned down the chance to have a beautiful woman in my arms," he said.

She flushed and Jackson almost grinned in satisfaction. He did so love making women blush and with Annabelle it seemed so easy. But he couldn't quite grin. He was working too hard on not giving away how much he wanted to have her up against him.

What the hell was going on?

She smiled and the feeling got stronger.

"Great." She started for the dance floor without waiting for him.

Jackson took a second to watch her go and changed his mind about not liking the flowing skirts. They weren't as good as yoga pants or nothing at all, of course, but there was something about the way the silky material draped over her hips, and swung against then away from the curve of her ass, that made a man's heart rate pick up.

It was kind of like the difference between flirting and outright telling a guy "I want you".

The blatant "I want you" was very, very nice. But a good flirtation was equally compelling once in a while.

Jackson glanced at the other men at the bar. None were watching Annabelle walk away.

That was good.

He thought he might want to keep the secret of Annabelle's cute butt to himself.

Jesus. Cute butt?

Jackson started after her. When she got the edge of the dance floor, she swung to face him and the skirt swirled around her.

Jackson noticed her boots immediately. Annabelle might have spent her teen years in tennis shoes but she was still a Texas girl and eventually they all wore cowboy boots. These were red though. Blood red. That did surprise him a bit though.

"Damn. Was hoping to catch a glimpse of that music thing again." He stepped close and held out his arms, palms up, ready to two-step her around to some George Strait.

"Music thing?"

"Your tattoo."

"The one on my foot?"

He lifted an eyebrow. "Is there another one?" *Oh, damn, please let there be another one.*

"There is. In fact, there are several more."

Yes. Now to convince her to show him where. "Several?"

She grinned. "Yes."

She still wasn't getting closer. He wiggled his fingers. "I'm not used to women taking so much time to get up against me," he told her. "I feel like a dumbass here, Annabelle. Come on."

She blinked, then seemed to register what he was talking about. She laughed, said, "Sorry," and stepped into his arms.

His hand settled on her lower back, hers on his shoulder as he took her other hand in his. They began moving in the steps that every kid in Quinn knew from the time they could walk. A country two-step was right up there with learning the Pledge of Allegiance and their bedtime prayers.

They began swaying and he just looked at her. Annabelle Hartington smelled like cupcakes.

Finally she asked, "What?"

"Shh," he told her. "I'm imagining your other tattoos."

She looked startled for a moment, then her face relaxed into a knowing smile that women have been giving men since the Garden of Eden. It was a mix of fake innocence and I've-got-you-right-where-I-want-you.

Which made something hot throb deep inside Jackson. He was right where she wanted him? She wanted him *anywhere*?

"What about them?" she asked sweetly.

But he was starting to suspect there was a spicy side to Annabelle.

He tightened the arm around her, pulling her closer. "What they are. Where they are."

162

She licked her bottom lip. "Why don't you just ask me?"

"My imagination is a lot of fun."

He was flirting with her. That wasn't exactly a shock. Jackson usually had to try *not* to flirt when he was dancing with women in bars. No, the surprising thing was that Annabelle seemed to realize it.

She certainly didn't strike him as the flirtatious party-girl type. Yet there was a recognition in her eyes that said she knew exactly what was going on.

And didn't mind a bit.

Annabelle tipped her head to one side, her lips curled in a soft smile and her body moved closer to his as the song switched to Brad Paisley's soft ballad *She's Everything.*

"I can almost guarantee," she said softly, "that you will never guess what the others are. And you will probably only guess *where* about half of them are."

Flirting had just ratcheted up to seduction. He was pretty sure. That's how this felt, anyway. The only thing making him wonder was the fact that this was Annabelle.

"How many are we talking?"

"Eight."

He knew his eyes went wide. "You have eight tattoos?"

She nodded. "Seven besides the one you've seen."

Of course they could be tiny. Little daisies didn't need to take up a lot of skin. But eight?

He'd dated women with tattoos before. Lots of them, in some cases. They were gorgeous and sexy and he loved them.

But there was something very sweetly sexy about Annabelle having seven other hidden tattoos that he really, really liked. Maybe it was because it was unexpected. But he thought maybe it was more that these tattoos were obviously only for her. She hadn't done it to be sexy—especially if the majority were hidden. She'd done it because she wanted to. They would say something about her.

He liked that most of all. And he *really* wanted to know what they were now.

His grip on her hand tightened and he dropped his voice to a husky growl. "I think instead of guessing, I'd rather go on a treasure hunt."

To read more about Out of Bounds and Erin Nicholas's other work, visit her website at www.erinnicholas.com

Free Agent
by Mari Carr

Tucker had only one aspiration in high school—to get the hell out of town the second that diploma was in his hands. The only way out was his talent as quarterback on the gridiron. And his plan worked. He turned pro his sophomore year of college and never looked back. Never had any regrets.

Except her. Lela and Tucker's romance had been like a force of nature—steamy, unstoppable and tempestuous. In her arms, Tuck could forget his troubled home life—until a family tragedy made him run, leaving Lela behind. For twelve years he's stayed away, unwilling to deal with his drunken father, his mother's death, and unable to face the girl he never stopped thinking about.

When Tucker gets a call that his high school coach has suffered a heart attack and needs help, he has to make a decision. Does he return with his teammates to help his beloved coach? Does he take the risk of running into his father? What does he say to Lela about the way he disappeared so completely?

And what if the spark that flared so hot between them still exists?

Excerpt:

"I'm afraid I…have…to…" She was searching for an excuse. And doing a terrible job at it.

He smirked. "You still suck at lying, L.B."

She shot him a dirty look. "Did you ever consider that I don't want to hang out with you and I'm looking for an acceptable reason, so that I don't hurt your feelings?"

He shook his head. "Nope. That thought never occurred to me. Because you're dying to go for a ride."

She rolled her eyes and started to walk away from him. "You cocky son of a b—"

Tucker had no idea what prompted his next move. Maybe it was because she was trying to get away. Or the adorable exasperation on her face. Or that damn smell that had his cock going hard in an instant.

Whatever it was, it had his hands on her upper arms, twisting her around to him, cutting off her words with hard, hungry lips.

Lela was motionless for several seconds. Tucker used her shock against her as he deepened the kiss. Her mouth had been open and he'd taken advantage of that fact, pressing his tongue against hers.

When she did move, Tucker tightened his grip and planted his feet to prepare, ready to halt her flight. But she didn't shove him away. Didn't turn her face away from his, didn't slap him for his forwardness.

Instead, she responded. Her lips softened and her tongue met his.

It was her turn to claim the advantage. She lifted her arms, wrapping them around his neck, her firm breasts pressed against his chest. Tucker released her arms, his hands dropping to her waist. He needed to touch her skin. He hadn't lived like a monk, hadn't resisted the perks associated with being a star quarterback. It wasn't unusual for beautiful women to invite him to their beds and he'd taken more than a few of them up on the offer.

He'd ventured into sex clubs and given in to dominant urges he'd never shown Lela when they'd been younger. He'd tied women up, down and sideways, but nothing, not one damn kinky, hot, sex-filled night, had turned him on more than this relatively simple kiss from Lela.

His hands drifted under her shirt. She shivered slightly when his fingers grazed her soft skin, despite the scorching heat.

Lela ran her hands through his hair before she closed her fingers in the strands, tugging it harder, using her grip to increase the pressure of the kiss.

Tucker didn't try to escape, didn't acknowledge the prickling pain in his scalp. There was a new roughness, an impassioned hunger to Lela's response. It spoke to Tucker's own needs.

With his hands on her hips, he twisted them, lightly pushing her back against the side of the car, stepping closer. He pressed his cock against her, letting her feel how hard he was, how much he wanted her. She whimpered, but didn't seek to break the union of their mouths.

Tucker was vaguely aware of their surroundings. They were in the front yard of a fairly busy ranch. Anyone and everyone could be watching them, but Tucker couldn't find it in himself to give a shit.

Besides, Lela was too pragmatic. Common sense was going to raise its ugly head soon enough and she'd definitely shove him away. Until then he had to make sure to leave a lasting impression. Take care to ensure this encounter wasn't something she'd soon forget.

His hands still lingered beneath her shirt. Lifting them, he wasted no time cupping her full breasts. He squeezed the flesh firmly, loving the way Lela moved toward the touch, encouraging him to continue.

They'd been virgins the first time they'd come together. Tucker had been so much bigger than her and he'd been terrified of hurting her. That fear had never left his young man's heart, so their sexual history had been steeped in gentleness and slow, easy lovemaking.

This older version of Lela was stronger, self-confident, sexy. Tucker couldn't offer her softness if his life depended on it. Instead, he felt the intense need to conquer. To prove to her she wasn't the only one who'd changed. To take her in all the ways he'd dreamed of on those lonely nights when he gave in and let himself fantasize about her.

She'd been the face he'd seen every time he'd closed his eyes, wrapped his hand around his cock and brought himself to climax. He'd envisioned her on her knees before him, her hands tied behind her back, sometimes blindfolded, sometimes not. She'd open her mouth upon his command and...

Tucker forced the sexy thoughts from his head before he really did do something neither of them was ready for.

To read more about Free Agent and Mari Carr's other work, visit her website at www.maricarr.com

WANT MORE SEXY SINGERS?

...or to find out more about Jazz and Gray who appeared in GOING LONG?

Check out my LOST IN OBLIVION rockstar series with Taryn Elliott!

LOST IN OBLIVION

the Series

SEDUCED (intro)
ROCKED (book 1)
ROCK, RATTLE & ROLL (book 1.5)
TWISTED (book 2)

Coming soon

UNTWISTED
DESTROYED
SHATTERED

If you'd like more information about the series & extras, please visit **www.lostinoblivion.com**

ABOUT THE AUTHOR

USA Today bestselling author Cari Quinn wrote her first story—a bible parable—in 2nd grade, much to the delight of the nuns at her Catholic school. Once she saw the warm reception that first tale garnered, she was hooked. Now she gets to pen sexy romances for a living and routinely counts her lucky stars. When she's not scribbling furiously, she can usually be found watching men's college basketball, playing her music way too loud or causing trouble. Sometimes simultaneously.

Visit her website at www.cariquinn.com and sign up for her NEWSLETTER or for some spicy fun, join her reader group with Taryn Elliott, the Word Wenches, on Facebook! https://www.facebook.com/groups/346424552124487/

Look for these titles by Cari Quinn

No Promises Required
Proving His Worth
Guarding His Heart
Protecting His Assets
Takedown
Shadowboxer

Find out more on www.cariquinn.com

www.ingramcontent.com/pod-product-compliance
Lightning Source LLC
Chambersburg PA
CBHW071520170626
46811CB00007B/2908